So lernst du mit Lighthouse

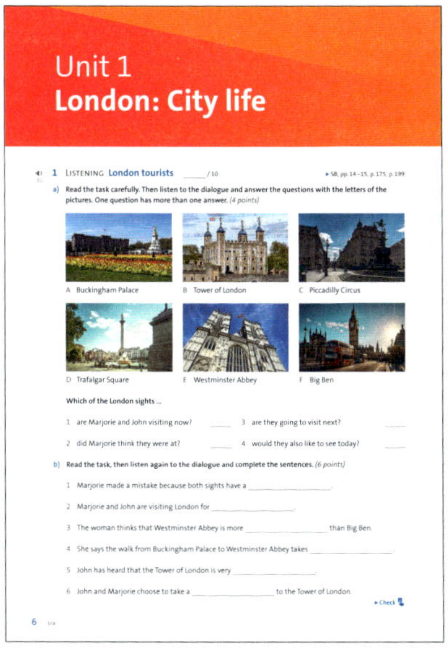

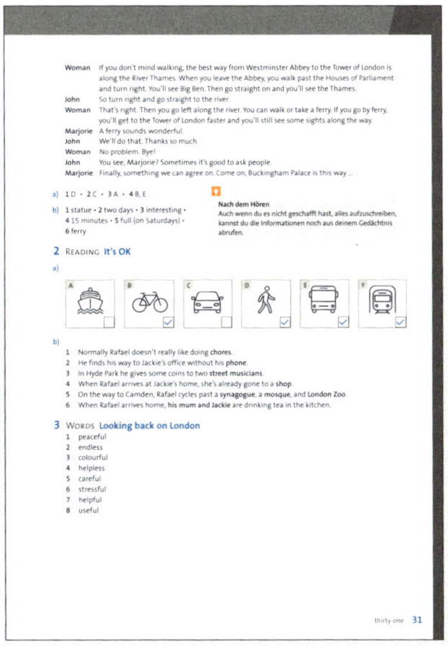

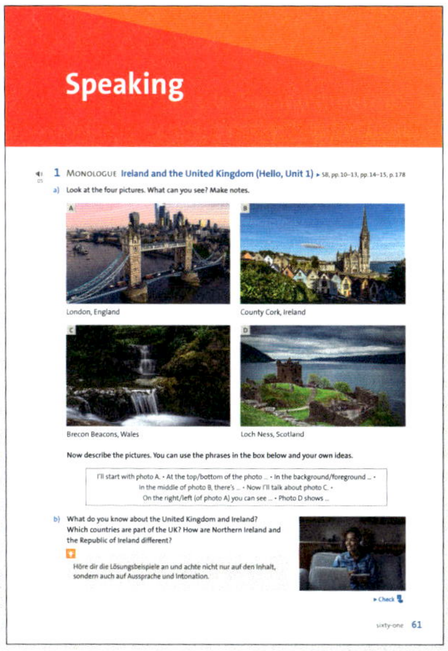

Dein Klassenarbeitstrainer hat fünf Units

In jeder Unit findest du Aufgaben zu verschiedenen Kompetenzen, die dich auf deine Klassenarbeit vorbereiten. Mit Hilfe der Tabelle am Ende jeder Unit kannst du deine Ergebnisse überblicken.

Überprüfe deine Lösungen

In der Mitte des Heftes findest du die Lösungen zu den Aufgaben. Hier findest du auch die Hörtexte, sowie Lerntipps, um dich optimal auf deine Klassenarbeit vorzubereiten.
Diese Seiten kannst du heraustrennen.

Sprechen üben

Vielleicht wirst du eine mündliche Klassenarbeit haben. Zwischen Units 4 und 5 findest du die *Speaking*-Unit. Hier kannst du Monologe und Dialoge üben.
Danach kannst du dir die Lösungsbeispiele anhören und deine Ergebnisse überprüfen.

Diese Symbole und Hinweise geben dir Orientierung

____/15

Neben den Aufgaben findest du die maximale Punktzahl. Dort kannst du deine erreichten Punkte eintragen.

► SB, p. 21, p. 183

Dieser Verweis zeigt dir, dass sich das Thema auf die Seiten 21 und 183 in deinem Schulbuch bezieht.

► More help, p. 73

Dieser Verweis führt dich zum *More Help*-Kapitel, wo du zusätzliche Hilfen für die *Writing*-Aufgabe findest.

Lerntipps zur Vorbereitung auf eine Klassenarbeit findest du auf den Seiten 78–79.

Deinen Klassenarbeitstrainer findest du auch in der Cornelsen Lernen App

Siehst du eines dieser Symbole in deinem Klassenarbeitstrainer, kannst du in deiner App …

Erklär-film

Hörtexte und Erklärfilme aufrufen.

► Check

deine Antworten überprüfen, falls du die Lösungsseiten nicht zur Hand hast.

ADVANCED lighthouse 3

Klassenarbeitstrainer

Im Auftrag des Verlages erarbeitet von
Marc Proulx, Berlin
und Katharina Pick, Wülfrath *(Vorwort, "So bereitest ...")*

In Zusammenarbeit mit der Englischredaktion
Klaus Unger (Projektleitung), Elizabeth Pancake-Steeg
und Chelsea Ledvinka-Heß, sowie Chiara Castellano

Lizenzmanagement
Silke Kirchhoff

Illustrationen
Gustavo Mazali, Beehive Illustration

Fotos
Anja Poehlmann, Brighton
Für die freundliche Unterstüzung danken wir
der *Varndean School, Brighton*

Umschlaggestaltung
Rosendahl, Berlin

Layoutkonzept
Klein & Halm, Berlin

Layout und technische Umsetzung
Compuscript Ireland and Chennai

Audio-Dateien
Studio
Clarity Studio, Berlin
Regie und Aufnahmeleitung
Susanne Kreutzer
Tontechnik
Dimitris Kritikos, Christian Schmitz

Druck
Athesiadruck GmbH

www.cornelsen.de

1. Auflage, 1. Druck 2024
978-3-06-034613-4

ADVANCED

lighthouse 3

Klassenarbeitstrainer

Deinen Klassenarbeitstrainer findest du auch in der **Cornelsen Lernen App**.

Siehst du eines dieser Symbole in deinem Klassenarbeitstrainer, findest du in der App …

- alle **Audios**
- alle **Erklärfilme**
- **Lösungen** zu den Aufgaben

Cornelsen

Vorwort für Eltern

Sie möchten Ihrem Kind ein sicheres Gefühl für die Klassenarbeiten geben?
Der Klassenarbeitstrainer hilft Ihrem Kind beim Lernen.

Dear Parents,

in den Klassenarbeiten Ihrer Kinder werden die Fertigkeiten Hörverstehen (*Listening*), Leseverstehen (*Reading*), Wortschatz (*Words*), Grammatik (*Language*), Mediation, Lernen lernen (*Study skills*) und Schreiben (*Writing*) abgefragt. Mit dem Klassenarbeitstrainer kann Ihr Kind diese Fertigkeiten gezielt trainieren. Für jede Unit finden Sie verschiedene Aufgaben zu den einzelnen Fertigkeiten.

Im Klassenarbeitstrainer finden Sie darüber hinaus ein Kapitel mit Übungen zur Fertigkeit Sprechen (*Speaking*).

Vorbereitung
Nicht jedes Thema aus dem Schulbuch ist für jeden Lehrplan und für jedes Bundesland relevant, vergewissern Sie sich daher, dass Ihr Kind sich mindestens eine Woche vor der Klassenarbeit genau über die relevanten Themen informiert. Mit einem Lernplan kann Ihr Kind festlegen, wann welche Fertigkeit geübt wird. Eine Vorlage dafür finden Sie auf Seite 79.

More help-Aufgaben
Schreiben stellt für Schülerinnen und Schüler eine besondere Herausforderung dar. Das Kapitel *More help* stellt zusätzliche Hilfen (*useful phrases, switchboxes, etc.*) für die *Writing*-Aufgaben zur Verfügung.

Speaking-Aufgaben
Zwischen den Units 4 und 5 finden Sie Übungen zur Fertigkeit Sprechen (*Speaking*). Manche dieser Übungen kann Ihr Kind allein bearbeiten, andere am besten mit einem Partner (z. B. Klassenkameraden). Damit Sie die Ergebnisse mit den Lösungsvorschlägen vergleichen können, sollte sich Ihr Kind beim Sprechen aufnehmen. Beispielhafte Antworten werden in diesem Klassenarbeitstrainer auch als Audioformat zur Verfügung gestellt.

Lösungen
Wenn eine Aufgabe bearbeitet wurde, kann diese mit den Lösungen aus dem herausnehmbaren Lösungsheft verglichen werden. Achten Sie beim Vergleichen genau darauf, welche Fehler gemacht wurden, und überlegen Sie mit Ihrem Kind, wie diese beim nächsten Mal vermieden werden können. Neben den Beispiellösungen enthält das Lösungsheft auch Lerntipps und die Skripte zu den Hörtexten. Die Bewertungstabelle am Ende jeder Unit hilft Ihnen dabei, den Lernstand Ihres Kindes besser einschätzen zu können.

Achtung
Natürlich enthält jede Unit mehr Aufgaben als eine normale Englischarbeit. Es ist also normal, dass Ihr Kind für die Bearbeitung einer Unit im Klassenarbeitstrainer länger braucht als für eine normale Arbeit.

Wir wünschen viel Spaß beim Lernen und eine erfolgreiche Klassenarbeit.
All the best

So lernst du mit Lighthouse 1

Impressum 2

Vorwort für Eltern 4

Inhaltsverzeichnis 5

Unit 1
London: City life 6

Unit 2
Manchester: Who we are 13

Unit 3
Scotland: Adventure 21

Lösungen 29

Unit 4
Wales: Digital life 53

Speaking 61

Unit 5
Two Irelands: Together 67

More help 73

So bereitest du dich auf eine Arbeit vor 78

Quellenverzeichnis 80

Übersicht Audio-Tracks U3

Unit 1
London: City life

1 Listening London tourists ______ / 10

01

► SB, pp. 14–15, p. 175, p. 199

a) **Read the task carefully. Then listen to the dialogue and answer the questions with the letters of the pictures. One question has more than one answer.** *(4 points)*

A Buckingham Palace

B Tower of London

C Piccadilly Circus

D Trafalgar Square

E Westminster Abbey

F Big Ben

Which of the London sights ...

1 are Marjorie and John visiting now? ______

2 did Marjorie think they were at? ______

3 are they going to visit next? ______

4 would they also like to see today? ______

b) **Read the task, then listen again to the dialogue and complete the sentences.** *(6 points)*

1 Marjorie made a mistake because both sights have a ____________________.

2 Marjorie and John are visiting London for ____________________.

3 The woman thinks that Westminster Abbey is more ____________________ than Big Ben.

4 She says the walk from Buckingham Palace to Westminster Abbey takes ____________________.

5 John has heard that the Tower of London is very ____________________.

6 John and Marjorie choose to take a ____________________ to the Tower of London.

► Check

2 READING It's OK ______ / 12

▸ SB, pp. 16–17, pp. 28–29, p. 176

Skimming und *Scanning* sind Lesestrategien, die dich bei bestimmten Fragestellungen unterstützen können. *Skimming* hilft dir, einen schnellen Überblick über den Inhalt eines Textes zu bekommen. Dafür schaust du dir z. B. **Überschriften**, den **ersten Satz** jedes Absatzes, sowie den **letzten Absatz** des Textes an. *Scanning* hilft dir nach bestimmten Informationen zu suchen. Überfliege den Text und suche nach einem bestimmten **Stichwort**. Lies die Textstelle, die dein Stichwort enthält, um zu sehen, ob du dort die Informationen findest.

a) **Read the text. Which types of transportation does Raffi use? Tick (✓). There are two pictures you don't need.** *(4 points)*

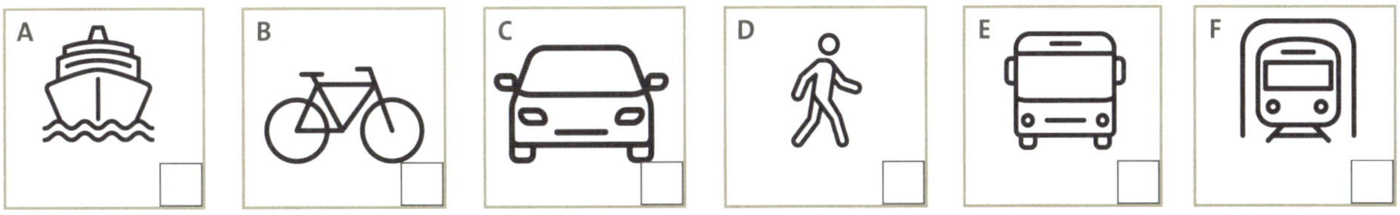

'Raffi, could you go pick something up for me?'
'Sure, Mum,' I said. This was one chore I didn't mind doing. I had to go see her friend Jackie at her office in South London.
At the tube station I took the escalator down to the platform and waited for the train. I soon discovered that my phone wasn't in my pocket or in my rucksack – it was still at home. But I didn't want to go back. I had the office address in my head, so when the train arrived, I got on.
At Leicester Square I changed to the Northern Line. Looking at all the people with their eyes stuck to their phones, I felt strangely free. I came out of the Waterloo tube station and walked along a busy road to a tall skyscraper, where I took a lift up to the 11th floor.
'Oh, sorry! Jackie just left 15 minutes ago,' an assistant said. 'She's on her way home.'
'It's OK,' I said. I knew where Jackie lived – it was in Notting Hill – and I knew a way there.
Back on the street, I saw a red double-decker bus with 'Hyde Park' on it. It was the right way, so I jumped on. As the bus crossed Westminster Bridge, I looked up the river at the London Eye, that big wheel turning in the sun.
At Hyde Park I got off the bus. If I walk fast, it won't take long, I thought. The trees were big and colourful. People were on bikes and skates and even horses. There were picnics, birthday parties, yoga groups and cricket games. Near Serpentine Lake two street musicians played guitar and drums for a small audience. I listened and put some coins in their hat. They smiled.
When I got to Bayswater Road, I used my bank card to hire a public bike. I enjoyed cycling the last 10 minutes to Notting Hill. Jackie's flat was easy to find. Her son Liam answered the door.
'She's just left,' he said. Not again, I thought. 'She's cycling to Greene's, a shop in Camden,' he said. 'If you hurry, maybe you'll catch her.'
I rode fast along the sleepy canals of Little Venice, past a synagogue and a mosque, through Regent's Park and past London Zoo. My legs were tired when I finally arrived.
I left the bike at Camden Market and, after looking at a cool T-shirt stall, found Greene's.
'You're the first person to come in today,' the shop lady said. That was good news. I crossed the road to a café to wait and watch for Jackie.
'Hey, Rafael!' someone said. It was Mel and Kofi, two school friends. I sat down and chatted with them. Then I saw Jackie riding away on her bike. I ran after her and called … but lost her in the traffic. Disappointed, I said goodbye to Mel and Kofi and went home on the tube.
When I opened the door, I heard Mum.
'Is that you, Raffi? Where've you been?'
'Sorry, Mum,' I said, walking into the kitchen. 'I missed her three times. I just couldn't …'
Mum and Jackie looked up from their tea.
'No, we're sorry,' Mum said. 'I tried calling you.'
'Oh,' I said. I thought about the day. 'It's OK.'

▸ Check

b) **Complete the sentences.** *(8 points)*

1 Normally Rafael doesn't really like doing ____________________.

2 He finds his way to Jackie's office without his ____________________.

3 In Hyde Park he gives some coins to two ____________________.

4 When Rafael arrives at Jackie's home, she's already gone to a ____________________.

5 On the way to Camden, Rafael cycles past a ____________________, a ____________________ and ____________________.

6 When Rafael arrives home, ____________________ are drinking tea in the kitchen.

3 WORDS Looking back on London ____/8

▸ SB, p. 25

Some classmates are sharing comments about the class trip to London in their online group chat. Complete their comments by using the words in brackets to make a word with *-less* or *-ful*.

That afternoon in Regent's Park was so ______________ (1 peace). I forgot that we were in the middle of London!

Do you remember that long, straight road that goes to Buckingham Palace? It was ______________ (2 end)!

Those big, ______________ (3 colour) electronic signs at Piccadilly Circus were really cool.

Mr Rollins looked so ______________ (4 help) when he couldn't get through the ticket gate at the tube station!

I remember we had to be really ______________ (5 care) crossing the street. So much traffic!

Yeah. I understand why people say that London can be very ______________ (6 stress).

I thought that Greg, the guy at our hostel, was so nice and ______________ (7 help).

And the Travelcards were really ______________ (8 use) for getting around the city.

▸ Check

Erklärfilm

4 LANGUAGE Traveller's tips ______ / 14

▸ SB, pp. 20–23, p. 187

Nola and Arun are going to London for the weekend, so they go online and find some tourist tips. Complete the tips with the correct verb forms of the conditional sentence type 1.

!

Conditional sentence type 1 besteht aus zwei Teilen: einem Nebensatz mit *if (if-clause)* im *simple present*, und einem Hauptsatz *(main clause)* mit *will*, *'ll* oder *won't*.

1 You ________________ (see) more of the city if you ________________ (hire) bikes.

2 If you ________________ (like) book shops, you ________________ (find) some great ones there.

3 You ________________ (get) everywhere faster if you ________________ (travel) by underground.

4 If you ________________ (take) the Rock Walking Tour, you ________________ (learn) about London's music history.

5 If you ________________ (not, see) The Lion King while you're in London, you ________________ (miss) a great show.

6 Camden Market ________________ (be) too busy if you ________________ (go) on a Saturday afternoon.

7 If you ________________ (enjoy) big slides, the Orbit Slide in Queen Elizabeth Olympic Park ________________ (not, disappoint) you.

Erklärfilm

5 LANGUAGE A royal visit ______ / 12

▸ SB, pp. 16–17, p. 185

Complete the text with the correct simple past form of the verbs in brackets.

Tom (1) ________________ (follow) the directions in Bela's text message. At the traffic light he (2) ________________ (turn) left on Westminster Bridge Road and (3) ________________ (go) straight across Westminster Bridge, past Big Ben and past the statue of Winston Churchill. When he (4) ________________ (get) to St James's Park, he (5) ________________ (take) the first right into the park. It (6) ________________ (be) a beautiful spring day.

He (7) ________________ (ride) his bike around the park lake to St James's Cafe on the other side. There he (8) ________________ (find) Bela sitting on a bench. They (9) ________________ (order) cold drinks and (10) ________________ (watch) the people. 'How many royal parks have we hung out in?' Tom (11) ________________ (ask). 'This is our third. Next week we'll go to Hyde Park. Then we have five more,' Bela (12) ________________ (say).

▸ Check

6 MEDIATION **Taking the tube** ______ / 8

▸ SB, pp. 16–17, pp. 22–23, p. 177

Leonie and her aunt are at Euston Station in London. They go to an information desk to get directions. Leonie's aunt doesn't speak English very well. Complete their conversation.

Leonie Excuse me, we want to go to the River Thames. Is this the right train line?

Woman If you tell me where on the Thames you want to go, I'll tell you which line you should take.

Aunt Was hat sie gesagt?

Leonie Wenn wir (1) ______________________________

____

Aunt Wir wollen das Shakespeare-Theater besuchen. Wie heißt es? Globe Theatre. Und dann den Tower of London.

Leonie (2) ______________________________

Woman I suggest you take the Northern Line five stops to Embankment, then change to the Circle Line and go east two stops to Blackfriars Station. You can walk from there. That's the most interesting way.

Leonie Sie meint, wir sollen (3) ______________________________

____

Woman You can walk across the Millenium Bridge and look at the river. It's very beautiful. And the Globe Theatre is close to the bridge.

Leonie (4) ______________________________

____

Aunt Ach, das hört sich schön an. Weiß sie, wie lange wir zu Fuß brauchen vom Theater zum Turm von London? Den Namen auf Englisch habe ich schon wieder vergessen.

Leonie (5) ______________________________

Woman It takes about 25 minutes. It's a very nice walk along the river.

Leonie (6) ______________________________

____

Aunt Noch eine Frage: Weiß sie, was die Eintrittskarten für den Turm von London kosten?

Leonie One more question: (7) ______________________________

Woman Yes. Tickets for adults are 35 pounds and for kids under 15 they're 17 pounds.

Leonie (8) ______________________________

Aunt Tja, nicht billig. Aber egal. Let's go!

▸ Check

7 WRITING **A class trip** ______ / 15

► More help, p. 73 ► SB. p. 27, p. 180

Write a blog post about a class trip that you have taken. Write 80 words or more.

- Find a title for your blog post
- Beginning: Introduce yourself and say where you went, when and for how long. Describe the weather.
- Middle: Pick three places/sights or activities and describe them. Make a new paragraph for each.
- End: Finish with a thought or message about your experience.

These questions can help you:
- How did you get there?
- How did you feel?
- Who was with you?
- Where did you stay (if you were there longer than one day)?
- What did you do/see/watch?

You can start like this:

Hi everyone. My name is ______

I want to tell you about ______

► Check

8 WORDS An exciting place ______/11

▸SB. pp. 16–23, pp. 28–29

Read this text from a travel article about visiting London. Complete the text with words from the box. There are three words that you don't need.

bench • crossed • direct • doorkeeper • followed • hired • instead • opposite • out and about • public • sights • suggested • traffic • Travelcards

When we left our four-star hotel, the friendly (1) ______________ smiled and said, 'Have a nice day!' I asked him the best way to get to Covent Garden. He (2) ______________ that we use (3) ______________ transport. He pointed to a bus stop (4) ______________ the hotel. We (5) ______________ the road and used our (6) ______________ to ride bus number 74 to London's West End. We wanted to get off at Piccadilly Circus but the (7) ______________ was slow, so (8) ______________ we got off at Oxford Circus and (9) ______________ the signs from there to Covent Garden. It was exciting to be (10) ______________ in this busy city with so many interesting (11) ______________ to see.

Bereich	Aufgabe	erreichte Punktzahl				
listening	1	_____ / 10	10–9	8	7–5	4–0
reading	2	_____ / 12	12–11	10–9	8–6	5–0
words	3 8	_____ / 8 _____ / 11 } _____ /19	19–18	17–14	13–10	9–0
language	4 5	_____ / 14 _____ / 12 } _____ /26	26–24	23–19	18–13	12–0
mediation	6	_____ / 8	8	7–6	5–4	4–0
writing	7	_____ / 15	15–14	13–11	10–8	7–0
Gesamt		_____ / 90	90–81	80–63	62–45	44–0

Unit 2
Manchester: Who we are

1 LISTENING My clothes ______ / 11

02

► SB, pp. 50–52, p. 175

a) **Will is talking to two students, Daisy and Markus, for the school podcast. Look carefully at the pictures and find the differences. Then listen to the dialogue and tick (✓) the boxes that show what Daisy and Markus are wearing.** *(2 points)*

Daisy

A

☐

B

☐

C

☐

Markus

A

☐

B

☐

C

☐

b) **Read the statements. Then listen again and complete them.** *(9 points)*

1 Will starts by talking about Daisy's and Markus's ____________________.

2 Daisy chose everything that she's wearing except for her ____________________.

3 When Markus first saw his shirt, he ____________________ with it.

4 Will doesn't want to talk about his ____________________ and ____________________.

5 When Markus bought his shirt in a ____________________ shop, he saved money and helped the ____________________.

6 Sometimes Daisy likes to ____________________ old jeans herself to make shorts, for example.

7 Markus says one way to save money is to ____________________ clothes with friends.

► Check

2 Reading The big game ______ / 8

▸ SB, pp. 62–65, p. 176

Read this article from Wheatley High School's student newspaper.

Vor dem Lesen: Schaue dir die Aufgaben zum Text an und achte auf Schlüsselwörter. Überlege dir, was du tun sollst und welche Lesestrategie gefordert ist.

a) **Tick (✓) the best title for the article.** *(1 point)*

1 ☐ Easy win for Wheatley

2 ☐ Burnham wins, no fan conflicts

3 ☐ Wheatley loses the Cup

4 ☐ Fans fight as Wheatley wins

5 ☐ A big win for Wheatley

6 ☐ Burnham too strong for Wheatley

On Friday afternoon at Wheatley Stadium the boys' football team faced Burnham High School, the number one team in Manchester. Last year the match against Burnham ended 3-2 when Burnham scored in additional time. That match was very disappointing for our boys. On Friday, Wheatley's trainer, Andreas Klein, said, 'We haven't forgotten it. We're confident that we can win this time'.

In the first half of the match, both teams played well. Burnham scored first when Manu Diallo put the ball in the net in the ninth minute. But five minutes later, Wheatley's Kyle Palmer hit the ball beautifully past Burnham's goalkeeper. The Wheatley fans cheered loudly. At half-time the score was 1-1.

The Wheatley school band came onto the pitch during the half-time break. They played the pop song *Why can't we be friends* because of last year's match, when there were fights between fans from the two schools. This time the fans from both schools clapped and sang together.

The second half began with a lot of mistakes by both teams. Wheatley's Amir Khan scored a penalty in the 61st minute. Wheatley had another chance to score ten minutes later, but Tim McGray missed a penalty. Then Burnham scored. At the end of 90 minutes, the score was 2-2, just like last year. But in additional time Wheatley's Diego Sanchez scored the match winner. The team ran onto the pitch and the Wheatley fans went crazy.

After the match, Andreas Klein said, 'We can be proud of ourselves. The second half was a bit

messy, but our team showed a lot of confidence. If we keep playing like this, we can win the Trafford Cup this year'.

Organizers said that there weren't any big conflicts between fans this year. Sport teacher Ann Pratchett said, 'There were a few nasty words and some of the Burnham fans called the Wheatley fans names, but most of the time it was peaceful. My compliments to the fans and the organizers. Well done, everyone!'

▸ Check

b) **Read the article again and answer the questions.** *(7 points)*

1 How did last year's match between the two teams end?

____

2 How did the Wheatley team feel before this year's match?

____

3 What happened in the first half of the match?

____

4 Why did the fans clap and sing during the half-time break?

____

5 What was the main difference in the second half of the match compared to the first half?

____

6 How did Wheatley's trainer describe the second half and the way his team played?

____

7 What were the two big differences between last year's match and this year's?

____

3 WORDS Voices of Manchester ____ /9

► SB, pp. 229–238

Read and complete the mini-dialogues with the correct word or words. The first letter of each word is given.

1 – I'm from Brighton. Manchester is new for me. What about you?
– I've always lived here. This is my h__________.

2 – Over here, Mum! I'm in the q__________ for tickets!
– Yes, yes, you don't have to s__________. I can see you and hear you.

3 – We have four new t__________ on our car. But what do we do with the old ones?
– Don't t__________ a__________ things like that. You can recycle them.

4 – Why do you hang out with her? She always says bad things about you.
– I know. She was a friend for a long time, but now she's more like a f__________.

5 – It must be annoying for you as a designer when people c__________ your ideas.
– I don't mind it. When they wear my fashions, they're paying me a c__________!

6 – She helps her brother a lot with his homework.
– That's because he has a learning d__________ and needs more time and support.

► Check

Erklär-film

4 LANGUAGE The things they said ______ / 6

▶ SB, pp. 55–57, pp. 188–189

Mira couldn't be there when her friends met at the weekend, so her friend Allie is telling her what they talked about. Read what the friends said and use the words and phrases in the box to complete Allie's texts to Mira. There are two more words or phrases than you need.

!

Um zu sagen, dass jemand etwas nicht tun darf, verwendest du *can't* oder *mustn't*. Bei Erlaubnissen und Verboten kannst du auch *(not) be allowed to* verwenden.

be allowed to / not be allowed to • have to / not have to • must / mustn't • should / shouldn't

My mum says I can't watch TV or check my phone if I haven't finished my homework.

1 Liz ______________ watch TV or check her phone until she's done her homework. Strict!

We have a great friendship. Claire always understands exactly what I mean.

2 Ross says he ______________ ______________ explain things to Claire. She understands him. Awww.

Mira is so good at volleyball. We need her on the team!

3 Liz thinks that you ______________ join the volleyball team.

If I don't study for the test on Monday, I'll be in big trouble.

4 Ethan ______________ study for the test. He can't meet tonight.

My parents don't mind if my brother and I play video games until late on Saturdays.

5 Ross and his brother ______________ play games until late on Saturdays. Lucky!

Just don't tell Mira what I said about her!

6 Ethan says that I ______________ tell you what he said ... Oops!

5 LANGUAGE Be kind! ______/7

▸ SB, pp. 58–59, p. 190

Sadie is speaking on her teen podcast about how teens can become more confident. Complete her statement with words from the box. There is one more word than you need.

each other • herself • itself • myself • ourselves • themselves • yourself • yourselves

I watched how my sister slowly lost confidence in (1) ________________. We talked a lot and that helped her feel better. After that I told (2) ________________ I can help other kids too. That's why I started this podcast – because so many teens don't believe in (3) ________________. I don't earn any money from the podcast, but it has helped so many people that it easily pays for (4) ________________. Our experiences teach us a lot about (5) ________________ and if we share what we've learned, we can support (6) ________________. My best advice is this: you are normal and nobody is perfect, so be kind to (7) ________________.

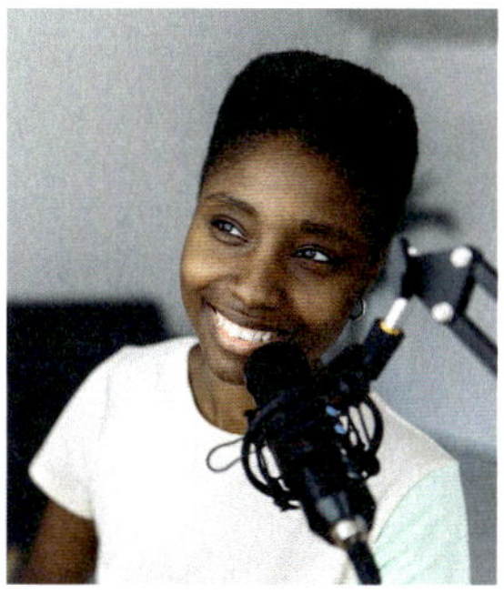

6 LANGUAGE Thoughts about fashion ______/8

▸ SB, p. 50, pp. 187–188

Trent likes to share his thoughts about fashion in his weekly fashion blog. This week he's comparing two outfits. Look at the pictures and complete his statements with comparatives or superlatives. You will also need *than*, *as* … *as*, and *not as* … *as*.

Here you can see my friends Holly and Abdul. Holly's outfits always look ________________________ (1 colourful) anybody else's. And she often has the ____________________ (2 crazy) hair styles that I know. I love how her hair is ____________________ (3 pink) her tights. An amazing match! You don't see this kind of fun look very much in Manchester, but it's quickly getting ____________________ (4 popular). Abdul's outfit is ____________________ (5 not, trendy) Holly's, but I think it's ____________________ (6 cool). The white t-shirt and jean jacket are ________________________ (7 traditional) Holly's outfit and I like that. And his boots are ________________________ (8 not, expensive) you might think. In fact, both outfits are amazingly cheap.

7 MEDIATION It's not fair ____ / 7

▸ SB, pp. 54–57, p. 177

Your friend Maya sees an interesting advice column in an online teen magazine. But her English isn't so good, so she sends you a link together with some questions. Read the column and answer her.

Dear Amber,

Thank you for your letter. I can certainly understand that you're annoyed when your older brother is allowed to do things that you're not allowed to do. I feel this too with my older sister. Sometimes I think my parents are being unfair. You say that your brother gets more social media time and more pocket money. My older sister is allowed to stay out later than me at the weekend.

But I think we needn't get too upset about it. Parents probably feel that there are things that an older kid is ready for and that a younger kid is not yet ready for. It doesn't feel right to us, but maybe for them it's not about what's fair or unfair. It's about keeping us safe in a dangerous world.

One day we'll be older too. Then we'll be allowed to do more.

Best wishes,
Nate

1 Maya: Moment. Warum ist Amber genervt?

Du: ______________________________

____

2 Maya: Und was wirft Nate seinen Eltern manchmal vor?

Du: ______________________________

3 Maya: Welche Beispiele gibt Amber?

Du: ______________________________

____

4 Maya: Sein Beispiel habe ich nicht ganz kapiert. Was ist mit seiner älteren Schwester?

Du: ______________________________

5 Maya: Warum sollten wir uns nicht zu sehr darüber aufregen seiner Meinung nach?

Du: ______________________________

6 Maya: Worum geht es denn für die Eltern?

Du: ______________________________

____

7 Maya: Was wird eines Tages passieren?

Du: ______________________________

____

8 WRITING Good advice ______ / 15

▶ More help, p. 74 ▶ SB, pp. 54–57, p. 180

You are helping with the advice column for your school's online student newspaper. Read the letter and give the student some advice. Write 80 words or more. You can use the phrases in the box to help you.

www.student.support.example.net

Dear advice column,
I have a classmate who I like and who I've wanted to be friends with, but he wasn't interested. That's changed now. We're hanging out a lot and he's really nice to me. But here's the problem: I've heard that he has a crush on my sister. She's a year younger than us. If he's using me to get closer to my sister, then he's not really a friend. What can I do?
Unsure friend

Thank you for your letter. • I understand that it's a difficult / an unhappy situation for you. • I can see why you feel unsure about ... • You want to trust him, but ... • I think you should ... • Maybe you can ... • Try to ... • Have you tried ...? • My advice would be to ... • Best wishes • Good luck!

Dear Unsure friend,

9 WORDS Football and fashion ____ / 8

► SB, p. 50, pp. 62-64, p. 200

Look at the picture and write the word for the numbered things.

1 ______________________ shirt

2 ______________________ blue jacket

3 ______________________

4 ______________________

5 ______________________

6 ______________________

7 ______________________

8 football ______________________

Bereich	Aufgabe	erreichte Punktzahl	🤩	😎	🤔	😭
listening	1	____ / 11	11–10	9–8	7–6	5–0
reading	2	____ / 8	8–7	6–5	4	3–0
words	3 9	____ / 9 ____ / 8 } ____ /17	17–15	14–12	11–9	8–0
language	4 5 6	____ / 6 ____ / 7 ____ / 8 } ____ /21	21–19	18–15	14–11	10–0
mediation	7	____ / 7	7	6–5	4	3–0
writing	8	____ / 15	15–14	13–11	10–8	7–0
Gesamt		____ / 79	79–71	70–55	54–40	39–0

Unit 3
Scotland: Adventure

1 LISTENING A different path ______ / 14

03

► SB, pp. 94–96, p. 175

Tim and Malik got lost when they went hiking with their class near Ben Nevis. Their teacher found them and is now talking to them. Look at the pictures carefully before you listen to their conversation.

a) Number the pictures in the order in which the boys saw them. *(6 points)*

A

B

C

D

E

F

b) Answer the questions. *(8 points)*

1 When did the boys recognize that they were on the wrong path?

____

2 What was Tim's 'great idea'?

____

3 Which way did the boys go after they met the man and woman?

____

4 How long did they rest when they came out of the forest?

____

5 What did the boys do when they came to the river? *(2 items)*

____

6 What happened before they crossed the bridge? *(2 items)*

____

► Check

2 READING Girl on a horse ______ / 10

► SB, pp. 82–83, p. 176

Read this story about a family on holiday in the Scottish Highlands. Then do the exercise on page 23.

Nora and her mum sat drinking tea in the holiday house. Nora texted a friend while her mum read a magazine.

'That's sad,' her mum said finally.

'What is it?' Nora said.

'Oh, this article about strange stories from the Highlands. It says many years ago a family went horse riding near here. A girl around your age was in front of the others. There was a loud noise from a car and her horse started running. The girl screamed and the others tried to help her, but the horse was too fast. Her long red hair was the last thing they saw of her as the horse ran away. They looked for her the whole day and night, but they couldn't find her. The next morning they found the horse eating grass by a loch. But they never found the girl.'

'How strange,' said Nora. 'And tomorrow we're going to go horse riding.'

Nora's mum smiled. 'Oh, we'll be fine.'

Then Nora's dad and her brother Jake came in from outside.

'What are you two talking about?' her dad asked.

'About a –,' Nora started.

'About tomorrow!' her mum said, 'We're excited. Right, Nora?'

'Erm, yeah,' Nora said. 'Right.'

The next day it was cool and grey as the four rode their horses along a nature path. It took them across fields and along one side of Loch Shiel. Nora wanted to ride slowly, but this was boring for Jake.

'Hey Dad, let's take that path through the field!' Jake said.

Nora's dad looked over at her mum.

'You two go ahead,' she said. 'Nora and I will wait for you here by the water.'

Nora was happy to take a break. Jake and his dad turned and rode away. Nora and her mum sat quietly by the loch. Nora thought about the girl.

An hour later Jake and her dad still weren't back. Nora began to worry about them.

'They'll be back soon,' her mum said. A few minutes later they heard horses. Jake and her dad appeared on the path.

'You see? There they are,' Nora's mum said.

'That was so cool!' Jake said excitedly. 'There was a scary old castle. Nobody seemed to live there ...,' he said.

Nora felt uncomfortable. 'Can we go now?' she asked.

The four rode back the way they came.

'Jake, tell Nora about your friend,' her dad said as they rode. Nora looked over at Jake.

'It was just a girl at that old castle,' Jake said.

'A girl? You said nobody was there,' Nora said.

'That's what we thought. Then suddenly she was there, standing in the field – a girl around your age.'

'Where did she come from?' Nora asked.

'I don't know. She was alone, and she was scared of our horses. And then she was gone again.'

Nora was quiet. Then she had a crazy thought. She stopped her horse and looked at Jake.

'Did she have ....' She nearly couldn't say the words. '... long red hair?'

Jake turned to his sister. 'Oh. You saw her too, huh?' he said.

► Check

Complete the sentences.

1 ______________________ read about the girl in a ______________________.

2 The horse ______________________ away when it heard a ______________________.

3 The next day Nora and her family went ______________________.

4 Jake and his dad took a path ______________________ while Nora and her mum waited ______________________.

5 Jake was excited about a scary ______________________.

6 The girl who he saw there was ______________________ of their horses.

7 She also had ______________________ hair.

3 Words An amazing holiday ____/9

▸ SB, pp. 80–81, pp. 239–248

Jesse is posting photos from her holiday in the Highlands. Complete the texts with the correct word.

Our (1) t ___ ___ ___ is the best!

At our campsite I found this cute (2) c ___ ___ ___ ___ ___ ___ ___!

This is a nice (3) v ___ ___ ___ of the (4) c ___ ___ ___ ___ where we were.

Here's Loch Ness. I didn't know it's so (5) d ___ ___ ___ – 800 metres!

A very (6) n ___ ___ ___ ___ ___ path. I had to walk (7) c ___ ___ ___ ___ ___ ___ ___ ___!

They (8) r ___ ___ ___ ___ ___ ___ a hiker from a mountain (9) r ___ ___ ___ ___!

▸ Check

4 Words It means ... ______ / 8

▶ pp. 239–248

Match the words with the correct definition. There is one more definition than you need.

1 eventually	A something hard to understand or explain
2 fake	B an area of land between hills or mountains
3 fortunately	C in the end, after a long time
4 mystery	D a woman with magic powers
5 spot sth.	E set something down in one place
6 submarine	F not real
7 valley	G another word for 'luckily'
8 witch	H see something suddenly or when it's not easy to see
	I a boat that can travel underwater

Erklär-film

5 Language A long way down ______ /12

▶ SB, pp. 84–85, p. 190

Read about Rita and Myra's sports adventure. Make adverbs from the adjectives in the brackets.

'Have you ever done something like this? It's so much fun!' Rita said ________________ (1 excited). She was still wet from her last jump. 'N-No, I haven't,' Myra answered. 'It's easy. I'll show you.' Rita walked to the cliff. She climbed ________________ (2 quick) onto a big rock and looked down. Then she jumped and screamed ________________ (3 loud) all the way down. It sounded like she hit the water ________________ (4 hard). That was fun? Myra thought to herself. When Rita's head came up out of the water, she laughed. 'Come on! Don't be scared!' she called ________________ (5 happy) to Myra. 'Scared? No way!' Myra shouted. Then she thought ________________ (6 sad), 'Why didn't I go kayaking?' After a moment Myra moved ________________ (7 slow) towards the cliff and climbed ________________ (8 careful) onto the big rock. She looked out at the beautiful view, then she looked ________________ (9 nervous) at the water far below. She closed her eyes and thought 'I can do this.' Then she opened them and jumped. She fell ________________ (10 fast) towards the water. Then ________________ (11 sudden) she was deep underwater. When she came back up, Rita said, 'You did that really ________________ (12 good)!' Myra was proud of herself. 'It was easy!' she said.

▶ Check

6 LANGUAGE Interview with an adventurer ______/15

▶ SB, pp. 86–89, pp. 192–193

a) **Sam is interviewing Scottish sports adventurer Lucy Maclean for a school radio podcast. Put the words in the correct order and write down the questions and answers.** *(8 points)*

Sam (1) many / climbed / you / how / mountains / so far / have / ?

____

Lucy (2) mountains / about / climbed / have / 20 / I / .

____

Sam (3) have / yourself / ever / you / climbing / hurt / ?

____

Lucy (4) several / I / accidents / had / yes, / have / . But nothing too serious.

____

Sam (5) You have done a lot of adventure sports. yet / you / skydiving / tried / have / ?

____

Lucy (6) in / have / here / yes, / already / I / Scotland / skydiving / been / . It was exciting.

____

Sam (7) enjoyed / the / which / most / you / sport / have / ?

____

Lucy (8) favourite / has / my / been / skiing / always / . Especially here in Scotland.

____

Erklär-film

b) **Sam has more questions for Lucy. Read their conversation and fill in the gaps with *since* or *for*.** *(7 points)*

!
Verwende *since* zur Angabe des Zeitpunkts und *for* zur Angabe eines Zeitraums.

Sam You've always said that Inverness is your favourite place in Scotland.

Lucy It's my favourite place anywhere! I've been here (1) ______________ I was born.

Sam What makes Inverness so attractive for you?

Lucy It's been a centre for adventure sports in the Highlands (2) ______________ years and years. And I've known a lot of people here (3) ______________ I was a child.

Sam You've had an adventure sports shop here (4) ______________ about three years. How is that going?

Lucy It's going well! We've had over 3,000 happy customers (5) ______________ we first opened. I've wanted to have my own business (6) ______________ secondary school, so it's really a dream come true!

Sam That's cool. Well, we've wanted to have you on our podcast (7) ______________ a very long time, so this interview is a dream come true for us!

▶ Check

7 MEDIATION The legend of the Devil's Table

____ / 10

► SB, p. 83, p. 177

You're on holiday with your family in the Scottish Highlands. You meet a girl named Skye who tells you about local legends and stories. Then she asks about German legends. You want to tell her the story of the *Teufelstisch*, a strange group of rocks in a forest area called Hinterweidenthal. Read the text and write the main ideas of the story in English.

Einmal war der Teufel[1] im Hinterweidenthal unterwegs. Müde und hungrig, suchte er einen Platz, wo er rasten konnte, aber er fand keinen. Also nahm er ein paar große Steine und baute sich einen Tisch daraus. Als die Menschen im Tal den riesigen Tisch am nächsten Morgen sahen, waren sie erschrocken.
„Da hat der Teufel sein Mitternachtsmahl gegessen", sagten sie.
Ein junger Mann jedoch lachte über die Leute. Er glaubte nicht an den Teufel.
„Ich werde heute Nacht dorthin gehen und mit dem Teufel zusammen essen", sagte er im Scherz.
In der Nacht ist er dann zu dem Teufelstisch gegangen. Gegen Mitternacht haben die Menschen im Tal einen schrecklichen Schrei gehört. Den jungen Mann haben sie nie wieder gesehen.

[1] **Teufel** *devil*

Skye Do you know any cool German legends?

You There's one that I like. It's about a group of rocks called the Devil's Table. It goes like this:

____

____

____

____

____

____

____

____

____

____

____

____

► Check

8 WRITING **Nessie on camera** ____ / 15

▶ More help, p. 75 ▶ SB, pp. 82–85, p. 180

Last weekend the MacDonalds from Glasgow went camping at Loch Ness. Look at the pictures below. Write what happened to Iona, Jamie, Mr and Mrs MacDonald. Use linking words (*and, but, …*) and time phrases (*later, then, …*). Write 80 words or more.

You can use words from the box below or your own ideas.

arrive • campsite • dinosaur • film • happy • look for • mobile phone • put up • secretly • show photos • surprised • tent • unpack

Deine Geschichte klingt interessanter, wenn du Adjektive verwendest, um Personen, Orte oder Dinge zu beschreiben. Verbinde deine Sätze mithife von *linking words*.

You can start like this:

In the afternoon the MacDonalds arrived at the campsite, ____________________

____

____

____

____

____

____

____

____

▶ Check

9 WORDS A special place ____ / 10

▸ SB, pp. 90–91, pp. 239–248

Read this short article from a tour guide. Use the words in the box to complete the text. There are two words that you don't need.

before • countryside • deer • heather • interest • landscapes • make sure • plants • protect • serious • Scots • wild

Scotland's nature

If you've never been to Scotland (1) ______________ and you want to visit not just the cities but also the (2) ______________, then (3) ______________ that you bring your outdoor clothes and get ready to experience nature like nowhere else in the British Isles. Scotland's beautiful (4) ______________ and the many different (5) ______________ and (6) ______________ animals that grow and live here are possibly the country's biggest attraction – from colourful fields of purple (7) ______________, which local people know by the (8) ______________ name *fraoch*, to the largest (9) ______________ in the UK, the Red Deer, which live in the hills and valleys of the Highlands. But because so many visitors come to Scotland, it's especially important that we do all we can to (10) ______________ its amazing nature so that in the future many more people can enjoy it.

Bereich	Aufgabe	erreichte Punktzahl	🤩	😎	🤔	😭
listening	1	____ / 14	14–13	12–10	9–8	7–0
reading	2	____ / 10	10–9	8–7	6–5	4–0
words	3 4 9	____ / 9 ____ / 8 ____ / 10 } ____ /27	27–25	24–19	18–14	13–0
language	5 6	____ /12 ____ / 15 } ____ /27	27–25	24–19	18–14	13–0
mediation	7	____ / 10	10–9	8–7	6–5	4–0
writing	8	____ / 15	15–14	13–11	10–8	7–0
Gesamt		____ / 103	103–93	92–72	71–52	51–0

ADVANCED

lighthouse 3

Klassenarbeitstrainer

Lösungen

Cornelsen

Unit 1 London: City life

01

1 LISTENING London tourists

Hörtext

Marjorie	Are you sure, John? I think this is Piccadilly Circus.
John	No, Marjorie, this is Trafalgar Square. Look over there. That's the National Gallery.
Marjorie	I'm not so sure. I'm going to ask this woman. Excuse me.
Woman	Yes?
Marjorie	Is this Trafalgar Square?
Woman	Yes, it is.
John	I told you.
Marjorie	Well, I thought it was Piccadilly Circus because it has a statue too.
John	But this is a square, Marjorie, not a circus. It looks totally different. Right?
Woman	Erm, yes, that's right.
John	Thanks for your help.
Woman	No problem.
Marjorie	Just one more question: Does that road there go to Buckingham Palace?
Woman	No, it's the other one. That's the Mall. If you walk straight along there, you'll come to Buckingham Palace.
John	Great. Thank you. Let's go.
Marjorie	And after Buckingham Palace, what would you suggest we visit next?
John	Marjorie, I really don't think she wants to –
Woman	Hm. How much time do you have?
Marjorie	Well, that's the problem.
John	Yes. We're only here for two days.
Woman	Oh, I see.
John	So I thought after Buckingham Palace we could visit Big Ben.
Marjorie	What do you think?
Woman	Well ... Westminster Abbey is in the same area and I think it's more interesting than Big Ben. There's a lot more history there.
John	Oh. Do you think so?
Marjorie	You see, John? It's good to ask people.
John	Fine, OK. We'll go to Westminster Abbey instead, and then we –
Marjorie	How long does it take to walk there from Buckingham Palace?
John	I think we'll be fine, Marjorie. We have our phone apps.
Woman	It takes about 15 minutes.
John	Really? Doesn't it take longer?
Woman	No, it's quite close.
Marjorie	OK! Thank you very much. Let's go, John. The changing of the guards starts soon.
John	Just a second. Do you think we should visit the Tower of London? I've heard that it's very full on Saturdays.
Woman	Well, all the sights will be very busy today, so don't let that stop you. It's a very interesting place.
John	I see. And how –
Marjorie	I think we'll work it out, John. Come on.
Woman	How do you get there?
John	Yes.

Woman	If you don't mind walking, the best way from Westminster Abbey to the Tower of London is along the River Thames. When you leave the Abbey, you walk past the Houses of Parliament and turn right. You'll see Big Ben. Then go straight on and you'll see the Thames.
John	So turn right and go straight to the river.
Woman	That's right. Then you go left along the river. You can walk or take a ferry. If you go by ferry, you'll get to the Tower of London faster and you'll still see some sights along the way.
Marjorie	A ferry sounds wonderful.
John	We'll do that. Thanks so much.
Woman	No problem. Bye!
John	You see, Marjorie? Sometimes it's good to ask people.
Marjorie	Finally, something we can agree on. Come on, Buckingham Palace is this way ...

a) **1** D • **2** C • **3** A • **4** B, E

b) **1** statue • **2** two days • **3** interesting • **4** 15 minutes • **5** full (on Saturdays) • **6** ferry

Nach dem Hören
Auch wenn du es nicht geschafft hast, alles aufzuschreiben, kannst du die Informationen noch aus deinem Gedächtnis abrufen.

2 READING **It's OK**

a)

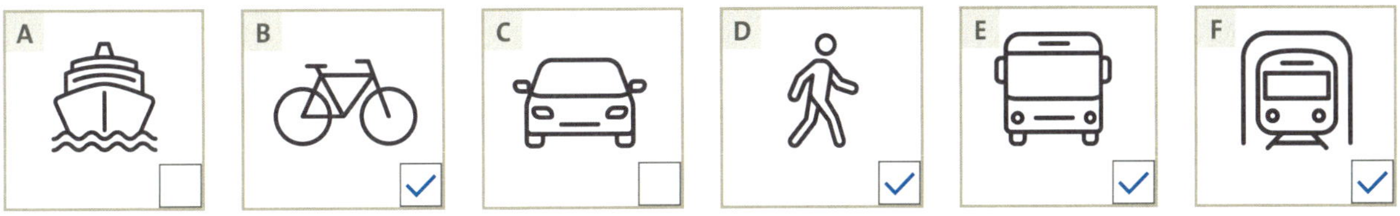

b)

1. Normally Rafael doesn't really like doing **chores**.
2. He finds his way to Jackie's office without his **phone**.
3. In Hyde Park he gives some coins to two **street musicians**.
4. When Rafael arrives at Jackie's home, she's already gone to a **shop**.
5. On the way to Camden, Rafael cycles past a **synagogue**, a **mosque**, and **London Zoo**.
6. When Rafael arrives home, **his mum and Jackie** are drinking tea in the kitchen.

3 WORDS **Looking back on London**

1. peaceful
2. endless
3. colourful
4. helpless
5. careful
6. stressful
7. helpful
8. useful

4 LANGUAGE Traveller's tips

1 You'**ll/will see** more of the city if you **hire** bikes.
2 If you **like** book shops, you'**ll/will find** some great ones there
3 You'**ll/will get** everywhere faster if you **travel** by underground.
4 If you **take** the Rock Walking Tour, you'**ll/will learn** about London's music history.
5 If you **don't see** The Lion King while you're in London, you'**ll/will miss** a great show.
6 Camden Market **will be** too busy if you **go** on a Saturday afternoon.
7 If you **enjoy** big slides, the Orbit Slide in Queen Elizabeth Olympic Park **won't/will not disappoint** you.

!

Mit Bedingungssätzen sagst du, was unter bestimmten Bedingungen geschehen wird.

Sie bestehen aus zwei Teilen:
• einem Nebensatz mit *if (if-clause)* im *simple present*, der die Bedingung nennt,
• einem Hauptsatz *(main clause)* mit *will, 'll* oder *won't*, der die Folge nennt.
If it rains tomorrow, we won't play football.

Der *if*-Teil kann auch **nach** dem Hauptsatz stehen:
We won't play football if it rains tomorrow.

5 LANGUAGE A royal visit

1 followed • **2** turned • **3** went • **4** got • **5** took • **6** was • **7** rode • **8** found • **9** ordered • **10** watched • **11** asked • **12** said

6 MEDIATION Taking the tube

(Lösungsbeispiel)

1 Wenn wir ihr sagen, wo wir an der Themse hingehen wollen, wird sie uns sagen, welche Zuglinie wir nehmen sollten.
2 We want to visit the Globe Theatre and then the Tower of London.
3 Sie meint, wir sollen die Northern Line fünf Stationen zu Embankment nehmen. Dann wechseln wir zur Circle Line und fahren zwei Stationen Richtung Osten zu Blackfriars Station. Von dort aus können wir laufen. Sie meint, das ist der interessanteste Weg.
4 Wir können die Millennium-Brücke zu Fuß überqueren und den Fluss anschauen. Sie meint, es ist sehr schön. Und das Theater ist nicht weit.
5 How long does it take to walk from the Shakespeare/Globe Theatre to the Tower of London?
6 Es dauert etwa 25 Minuten. Sie meint, es ist ein schöner Spaziergang (am Fluss entlang).
7 Do you know how much the tickets for the Tower of London cost?
8 Für Erwachsene kosten sie 35 Pfund und für Kinder unter 15 kosten sie 17 Pfund.

Achte in Gesprächen auf die Pronomen
Überlege immer, an wen du dich gerade wendest, und passe die Pronomen entsprechend an.

Ein Beispiel:
Frage Sam doch mal, wie ihm sein Tag gefallen hat.

Wenn du die Frage auf Englisch an Sam richtest wird es zu:
Did you enjoy your day?

7 WRITING **A class trip**

Benutze die Checkliste um zu kontrollieren, ob du die Aufgabe erfüllt hast. Hast du etwas über die folgenden Themen geschrieben? Gib dir drei Punkte für jedes Thema, das du erwähnt hast.

Did you ...		✓
find a title for your blog post?	Class trip to ... • Fun in ... • Amazing trip to ... • 7B in	
introduce yourself?	My name is ... • Hi, I'm ...	
say where you went and for how long?	We went to ... • We went by bus/train/car ... • We stayed in/at ... • We were there for ...	
write about three places/ sights or activities?	We went to ... • We saw ... • On the first/second/third day ... • First, we ... • In the morning/afternoon/ evening ...	
finish with a thought or message about your experience?	... was amazing! • I'm sure I'll go back. • I loved ... • It was ... • I think I'll ...	
	Total:	______/ 15

(Lösungsbeispiel)

Class trip to London

Hi everyone. My name is Vincent. I want to tell you about our class trip to London last spring. We were there for three days. The weather was cool and cloudy every day. We stayed in a hostel near Hyde Park. On the first day we took a tour of Buckingham Palace. It's so big! But we didn't see the King. The next day we did a boat tour on the River Thames and saw a lot of sights. On the last day we visited the Tate Modern, a big art museum. It was great. In the evening we went to the musical The Book of Mormon. It was funny and I understood a lot. London is amazing. I'm sure I'll go back again.

Überprüfe und korrigiere deinen Text
Mache nach dem Schreiben eine kurze Pause. Dann fange an, den Text inhaltlich und sprachlich zu verbessern. Prüfe:
- Hast du irgendwo ein Wort vergessen?
- Sind die Satze gut verstandlich?
- Ist die Reihenfolge der Satze sinnvoll?
- Hast du Absätze gemacht?
- Hast du *linking words* (Bindeworter) benutzt?
- Hast du Personen, Orte oder Dinge mithilfe von Adjektiven beschrieben?

8 WORDS **An exciting place**

1 doorkeeper • **2** suggested • **3** public • **4** opposite • **5** crossed • **6** Travelcards • **7** traffic • **8** instead • **9** followed • **10** out and about • **11** sights

Unit 2 Manchester: Who we are

02

1 LISTENING My clothes

Hörtext

Will Hey, everybody. It's Will here. Today we're talking about fashion with Daisy and Markus, who are both in year 10. First let's talk about what you're wearing. You both have really cool outfits. Daisy, what about your outfit?
Daisy This is more colourful than a lot of the outfits I wear. And you can see that I prefer baggy clothes.
Will So you're wearing a red skirt together with light green tights and black boots.
Daisy Yeah, red and green are trendy at the moment.
Will And you're wearing a baggy, dark green sweatshirt over the skirt.
Daisy Yes. And a black hat with an orange flower pattern.
Will I love it. Did you choose everything yourself?
Daisy Everything except for the hat. That was my dad's idea.
Will Oh, wow! Markus, your outfit isn't as colourful as Daisy's, but I like the patterned look.
Markus Yeah, some people think shirts with patterns are old-fashioned, but I disagree. I saw this shirt in a second-hand shop and I fell in love with it.
Will It's light blue with a dark blue pattern that looks modern, not at all old-fashioned. Especially together with those tight black trousers.
Markus Yeah, I know the baggy look is in style, but that doesn't work for me.
Daisy I love those blue and white basketball shoes, Markus.
Markus Thanks. And I like your boots, Daisy.
Will Yes. And we won't talk about my boring blue jeans and T-shirt. But I think we should talk about the problems with fashion. Markus, you said you bought your shirt in a second-hand shop.
Markus That's right.
Will That's a good example of fashion that saves money and helps the planet.
Markus Yeah, someone in our class gave a presentation about the clothing business and how it's really bad for the planet.
Daisy But sometimes we need to buy new clothes. What can we do?
Will But they don't always have to be new clothes. Like Markus, we can shop in second-hand shops, for example.
Daisy That's true. Sometimes I upcycle old jeans myself and make them into shorts or a skirt. The jeans get a new life and I get a new piece of clothing.
Will Cool! People should do more of that. There are so many ways to repair and reuse clothes.
Markus I've swapped clothes with friends before too. We helped each other and didn't have to spend any money.
Will I've done that with friends too. In fact, I think that's how I got this T-shirt!

Nutze die zahlreichen Möglichkeiten, um englische Texte zu hören. Wähle etwas aus, was dir gefällt, z. B. dein Lieblingslied oder dein Lieblingsbuch als Hörbuch auf Englisch. Schaue Filme oder Serien auf Englisch. Blende englische Untertitel ein, falls du Probleme beim Verstehen hast. Blende sie aus, wenn du dich sicherer fühlst oder eine Episode schon mehrfach gesehen hast.

a)

Daisy

A

B

C

Markus

A

B

C

b) **1** outfits • **2** hat • **3** fell in love • **4** (blue) jeans; T-shirt • **5** second-hand; planet • **6** upcycle • **7** swap

2 Reading The big game

a)

5 A big win for Wheatley

b)

1 Burnham scored in additional time and won 3–2.
2 The coach said they felt confident.
3 Both teams scored a goal.
4 The band played 'Why can't we be friends' after the fights at last year's game.
5 Both teams made a lot of mistakes.
6 The second half was a bit messy, but the team showed a lot of confidence.
7 This year Wheatley won and the fans were mostly peaceful.

3 Words Voices of Manchester

1 hometown
2 queue; shout
3 tyres; throw away
4 frenemy
5 copy; compliment
6 disability

Vokabeln kannst du immer und überall wiederholen. Für unterwegs kannst du sie dir aufs Handy sprechen oder mit einer Vokabeltrainer-App üben. Je öfter du die Vokabeln wiederholst, desto besser wirst du sie dir merken können.

4 Language The things they said

1 Liz **isn't allowed to / mustn't** watch TV or check her phone until she's done her homework. Strict!
2 Ross says he **doesn't have to** explain things to Claire. She understands him. Awww.
3 Liz thinks that you **should** join the volleyball team.
4 Ethan **has to** study for the test. He can't meet tonight.
5 Ross and his brother **are allowed to** play games until late on Saturdays. Lucky!
6 Ethan says that I **shouldn't / mustn't** tell you what he said ... Oops!

!

Mit *must* oder *have to* sagst du, was jemand tun muss.

Mit *don't / doesn't have to* sagst du, was jemand nicht zu tun braucht.

Bei Erlaubnissen und Verboten kannst du auch *be (not) allowed to* verwenden.

Mit *should / shouldn't* rätst du jemandem, etwas zu tun oder nicht zu tun.

5 Language Be kind!

1 herself • **2** myself • **3** themselves • **4** itself • **5** ourselves • **6** each other • **7** yourself/yourselves

!

Reflexivpronomen enden auf *-self* oder *-selves*. Du sagst damit, das jemand etwas selbst tut.
Each other entspricht „uns/euch/sich" im Sinne von „uns/euch/sich gegenseitig".
Vergleiche:
He smiled at me.
He smiled at himself (in the mirror).
We smiled at each other.

6 Language Thoughts about fashion

1 more colourful than
2 craziest
3 as pink as
4 (more and) more popular
5 not as trendy as
6 cooler
7 more traditional than
8 not as expensive as

!

Bei **einsilbigen** und bei **zweisilbigen** Adjektiven, die auf -y enden, hängst du *-er / -est* an das Adjektiv:

- *taller, funnier* (Komparativ = erste Steigerungsform)
- *(the) tallest, (the) funniest* (Superlativ = höchste Steigerungsform)

Bei **längeren** (vor allem **dreisilbigen**) Adjektiven setzt man *more / most* vor das Adjektiv:

- *more expensive* (Komparativ = erste Steigerungsform)
- *(the) most interesting* (Superlativ = höchste Steigerungsform)

7 Mediation It's not fair

(Lösungsbeispiel)

1 Es nervt sie, dass ihr älterer Bruder Dinge tun darf, die sie nicht tun darf.
2 Er wirf ihnen vor, dass sie unfair sind.
3 Ihr Bruder darf mehr Zeit in sozialen Medien verbringen und bekommt auch mehr Taschengeld.
4 Seine Schwester darf am Wochenende länger wegbleiben als er.
5 Wir sollten uns nicht zu sehr darüber aufregen, weil es für unsere Eltern Dinge gibt, für die ältere Kinder schon bereit sind, jüngere Kinder aber noch nicht.
6 Es geht ihnen darum, uns in einer gefährlichen Welt zu schützen.
7 Wir werden älter sein, und dann werden wir auch mehr tun dürfen.

8 Writing Good advice

Benutze die Checkliste um zu kontrollieren, ob du die Aufgabe erfüllt hast. Hast du etwas über die folgenden Themen geschrieben? Gib dir drei Punkte für jedes Thema, das du erwähnt hast.

Did you ...		✓
say thank you for the letter?	Thank you for writing to the advice column / for writing to us / for the letter.	
quickly explain the problem?	It's a bit strange that he ... • You want to trust him, but ... • If he ..., then maybe ... • You say that ...	
show understanding?	I can see why you feel ... • I see why you need advice. • I understand it's a difficult / an unhappy situation • It hurts when ...	
give useful advice?	Have you tried ...? • I think you should/shouldn't ... • Maybe you can ... • My advice would be ... • Try to ... • You could ...	
say goodbye?	Best wishes • Good luck!	

Total: ______/ 15

(Lösungsbeispiel)

Dear Unsure friend,

Thank you for writing to us. I can see why you feel unsure about the friendship with your classmate. It's a bit strange that he was never interested in being your friend before, but now he is. You want to trust him, but if he has a crush on your sister, then maybe that's why he wants to hang out with you. And that's not a good reason. I think you should be careful. Try to talk to him and find out how he feels about your sister and if he really wants an open and honest friendship with you. And get ready. Maybe you'll be disappointed.

Best wishes,

Senna

9 Words Football and fashion

1 patterned (shirt) • **2** plain/baggy (blue jacket) • **3** skirt • **4** tights • **5** goal • **6** goalkeeper • **7** net • **8** (football) pitch

Unit 3 Scotland: Adventure

03

1 LISTENING A different path

Hörtext

Mr Kumar	Tell me again slowly, boys. I want to know what happened.
Tim	Well, we didn't know that we were on the wrong path. Right, Malik?
Malik	Yeah. We walked for a long time.
Mr Kumar	But didn't you see that you were alone on the path?
Tim	No. We were in front of you guys.
Mr Kumar	I asked everybody to stay together. Remember? When did you see that you were on the wrong path?
Malik	After maybe 15 minutes. We stopped and waited for the others.
Tim	And hey, Mr Kumar! We spotted a big deer!
Malik	Yeah! It looked straight at us and ...
Mr Kumar	Forget about that now, boys. What about the group?
Malik	When you guys didn't come after ten minutes, we knew something was wrong.
Mr Kumar	Did you turn around and go back?
Tim	Erm, ...
Malik	No, we didn't.
Mr Kumar	I don't understand. Why not?
Malik	Well, Tim had this "great" idea.
Tim	OK, so it wasn't so great.
Malik	He thought we should stay on the path.
Tim	It looked like it went up and around the mountain. I thought we could meet the group at the other end.
Mr Kumar	But that's a long walk, Tim.
Malik	I thought so too. We walked for over an hour! Then we met a man and a woman. Americans.
Tim	I think they were Canadians.
Malik	No, I'm sure they were Americans because they –
Mr Kumar	Never mind. What did you do then, Malik?
Malik	They told us about a different path that went down the hill and through a forest and –
Mr Kumar	Through a forest? I hope you didn't –
Malik	... so we chose that path.
Mr Kumar	Ugh.
Tim	We walked for a really long time.
Mr Kumar	I'm sure you did.
Tim	We were tired when we came out of the forest, so we took another break.
Mr Kumar	Hm. How long?
Malik	About thirty minutes maybe. We saw those cool birds. Remember, Tim?
Tim	Yeah. I saw them first.
Malik	No, you didn't, I ...
Mr Kumar	And then?
Tim	Erm, then we hiked until we came to a river.
Mr Kumar	And then you turned left and went along the river?
Malik	That's right. It was beautiful there.
Mr Kumar	That's the River Dove. So you walked along the river path ...
Malik	Yeah, until we came to a small bridge.
Tim	I thought it was quite big.
Mr Kumar	Never mind, Tim. Which bridge?
Malik	Yeah, Tim. The sign said "Washgate Bridge".

Tim No, Wallgate Bridge.
Mr Kumar Malik's right, Tim. It's Washgate Bridge.
Tim Hm. I don't think so.
Mr Kumar OK. What did you do then? You crossed the bridge?
Malik Yes.
Tim No.
Mr Kumar Oh, come on, guys. Did you cross or didn't you?
Tim First we tried to catch that frog.
Mr Kumar That what?
Malik Oh, yeah! It was on a rock in the river! And I tried to –
Mr Kumar Ugh! Please. I don't care about fish right now.
Tim It was a frog.
Mr Kumar Fine! I'd like to know if you crossed the bridge.
Tim The big bridge. Yep. We did.
Mr Kumar And where did you go from there? Left or right?
Tim Erm, we turned ... right. We went through a gate and across a big field.
Malik Yes. A field with cows.
Tim Lots of cows. They looked like ...
Mr Kumar Are you sure you didn't turn left?
Malik Tim's right, Mr Kumar. We turned right.
Tim Hey – right, right!
Malik That's right, we turned right!
Mr Kumar Well, right was not right, boys. That was the wrong turn! Those people who you met – did they tell you to do that, too?
Malik Erm, ...
Tim Yeah, they did.
Mr Kumar Americans.
Tim I think they were Canadians.

Bleibe ruhig, wenn du beim ersten Mal nicht alles verstehst. Du hörst den Text meist zweimal.

a)

b)

(Lösungsbeispiel)

1 They knew (that they were on the wrong path) after 15 minutes.
2 Tim's great idea was to stay on the path/that they should stay on the path.
3 They went down the hill and through the forest.
4 They rested for about 30 minutes.
5 They turned left. They walked along the river path.
6 They saw a frog. They tried to catch it.

2 READING Girl on a horse

Je mehr englische Texte du liest, desto größer wird dein Wortschatz und desto schneller und besser verstehst du Texte.

1 **Nora's mum** read about the girl in a **magazine**.
2 The horse **ran** away when it heard a **loud noise**.
3 The next day Nora and her family went **horse riding**.
4 Jake and his dad took a path **through a field** while Nora and her mum waited **by the water**.
5 Jake was excited about a scary **old castle**.
6 The girl who he saw there was **scared** of their horses.
7 She also had **long red** hair.

3 WORDS An amazing holiday

1 tent
2 creature
3 view
4 coast
5 deep
6 narrow
7 carefully
8 rescued
9 ridge

Checkliste Vokabeln lernen

- Lerne nur 5–10 Vokabeln auf einmal.
- Lerne jeden Tag 10 Minuten.
- Lerne zusammen mit Freunden.
- Lerne unterwegs mit einer Vokabeltrainer-App.
- Schreibe schwierige Wörter mehrmals auf.
- Sprich die Wörter und nimm dich mit dem Handy auf.

4 Words It means ...

1 eventually	A something hard to understand or explain
2 fake	B an area of land between hills or mountains
3 fortunately	C in the end, after a long time
4 mystery	D a woman with magic powers
5 spot sth.	E set something down in one place
6 submarine	F not real
7 valley	G another word for 'luckily'
8 witch	H see something suddenly or when it's not easy to see
	I a boat that can travel underwater

5 Language A long way down

1 excitedly • **2** quickly • **3** loudly • **4** hard • **5** happily • **6** sadly • **7** slowly • **8** carefully • **9** nervously • **10** fast • **11** suddenly • **12** well

6 Language Interview with an adventurer

a)

1 How many mountains have you climbed so far?
2 I have climbed about 20 mountains.
3 Have you ever hurt yourself climbing?
4 Yes, I have had several accidents.
5 You have done a lot of adventure sports.
Have you tried skydiving yet?
6 Yes I have already been skydiving here in Scotland.
7 Which sport have you enjoyed the most?
8 Skiing has always been my favourite.

!

Mit dem present perfect kannst du auch sagen, wie lange etwas schon andauert. Dann verwendest du:

since zur Angabe eines Zeitpunkts:
since 3 o'clock, since May.

for zur Angabe eines Zeitraums:
for ten weeks, for two days.

b)

1 since
2 for
3 since
4 for
5 since
6 since
7 for

7 Mediation The legend of the Devil's Table

(Lösungsbeispiel)

Once the devil was walking around in Hinterweidenthal. Tired and hungry, he was looking for a place where he could rest, but he couldn't find one. So he took a few big stones and used them to build himself a table. When the people in the valley saw the enormous table the next morning, they were shocked. 'That's where the devil ate his midnight meal,' they said. One young man, however, laughed at the people. He did not believe in the devil. 'I'll go there tonight and eat with the devil,' he said jokingly. That night, he went to the Devil's Table. Around midnight, the people in the valley heard a terrible scream. They never saw the young man again.

8 Writing **Nessie on camera**

Benutze die Checkliste um zu kontrollieren, ob du die Aufgabe erfüllt hast. Gib dir drei Punkte für jede Frage, die du mit „ja“ beantwortest. Wenn du die Aufgabe nur zum Teil erfüllt hast, gib dir zwei Punkte.

Did you ...		✓
use the simple past?	arrived • put • unpacked • got • saw • showed • ...	
describe what happens in all five pictures?		
use at least 4 linking words?	and • because • but • first, second, ... • however • so	
use at least 3 words from the word box?	arrive • campsite • dinosaur • film • happy • look for • mobile phone • put up • secretly • show photos • surprised • tent • unpack	
write at least 80 words?		
	Total: ______/ 15	

(Lösungsbeispiel)
In the afternoon the MacDonalds arrived at the campsite. They put up their tent and were happy to be camping finally. Later Iona unpacked her toy dinosaurs and played with them. Jamie saw the dinosaurs and got an idea. He secretly took one that looked a bit like Nessie. He put it in the loch and took photos of it with his mobile phone. Then in the evening when they had dinner, Jamie said, 'Look what I saw!' He showed his parents and his sister the photos. They were very surprised. The next day Iona looked for her dinosaur toys, but one of them was missing. Then she thought of her brother's photos. 'Jamie!' she called.

Checkliste typische Fehlerquellen
- Groß- und Kleinschreibung
- unregelmäßige Pluralformen (child – children, man – men)
- gleicher Klang, aber unterschiedliche Schreibweisen und Bedeutungen (to – too – two, their – there – they're)
- Präpositionen (by train, in the picture, on the bus)
- unregelmäßige Verben (siehe Schulbuch, S. 272–273)
- Wörter mit stummen Buchstaben (climb, know)

9 Words **A special place**

1 before
2 countryside
3 make sure
4 landscapes
5 plants
6 wild
7 heather
8 Scots
9 deer
10 protect

04

1 LISTENING How are things?

Hörtext

Vor dem Hören
Lies dir die Aufgabenstellung genau durch und überlege, was du tun sollst. Finde die Schlüsselwörter in der Aufgabestellung. Geht es um ein allgemeines Thema oder um Details?

Beth Hi, Alfie. How are things?
Alfie Fine, thanks. I have a little problem, Beth, and I need your help.
Beth Are you talking about the maths homework for tomorrow?
Alfie No, it's something else. Do you remember those photos that I posted yesterday?
Beth The ones from your holiday in Wales? I loved those. That beach near Swansea looks beautiful.
Alfie Yeah, the beach was really nice, but ...
Beth You took some amazing photos, Alfie!
Alfie Yeah, ... that's the problem.
Beth Why? What is it?
Alfie I'd like to delete some of them. (breaking up)
Beth What? Sorry, I can't hear you. You're breaking up.
Alfie Can you hear me now? I said I'd like to delete some of those photos. I want to take them off my account completely, but I don't know how. I've never done that before.
Beth I can help you if you like. But why delete them? You've got so many likes.
Alfie Yeah, I'm hearing from a lot of people who've been to Wales.
Beth Hey, I've been to that lighthouse on Llanddwyn Island too! Did you climb up those old steps?
Alfie No, I didn't. Because I didn't go to the lighthouse.
Beth Wait. What? But you posted a photo from there.
Alfie I didn't take the photo. I found it online.
Beth But why did you do that, Alfie? You told me you had a great time in Wales!
Alfie It was nice. We had a good time. But my photos weren't as great as some of those amazing holiday photos that people are always posting.
Beth So you didn't go hiking in the Brecon Beacons?
Alfie Yes, we did! That was cool. We hiked almost 20 kilometres. The landscapes there were beautiful. I took that photo on the second day. But you know those sheep in the other photo?
Beth Yes. They're so cute.
Alfie We didn't see those. In fact, we didn't see a single sheep the whole holiday.
Beth No sheep? But you guys were in Wales!
Alfie I know. Amazing, right? I copied that photo from a travel website.
Beth Oh, Alfie.
Alfie Yeah, sorry. I feel terrible. And I'm embarrassed when people talk to me about the photos. I don't want to lie to them.
Beth But it was a lie when you posted them.
Alfie I know. It was stupid of me.
Beth When I saw the photo of Conwy Castle, I remembered when I was there with my grandma and grandpa. That's why I texted you. I was so excited that you were there.
Alfie That's another one from the travel website. I need to delete that too.
Beth What about the fans at the rugby match? Was that real?
Alfie Yes! That was really exciting.
Beth I'm so jealous. I would love to go to a big rugby match.
Alfie We should go together some time!
Beth It sounds like you had a cool holiday, Alfie, even if you didn't go to the lighthouse or Conwy Castle or see any sheep.

Alfie You're right. I need to stop worrying about what other people think. So Beth, could you help me delete those photos?
Beth Sure. Shall I come over and do it for you? Or do you want to do it yourself?
Alfie I can do it. Could you just tell me how?
Beth OK. First click on the photos that you want to ...

a)

A great rugby match!

These guys are everywhere! [x]

Beach day near Swansea!

Conwy Castle is so cool! [x]

Beauty in the Brecon Beacons

I love this little lighthouse! [x]

b) **1** c) • **2** c) • **3** b) • **4** a) • **5** c) • **6** b)

2 Reading **In a Welsh village**

a)

- 6 They drink tea and talk about the sheep farm.
- 2 Erin photographs some flowers.
- 7 Griff becomes quiet when he sees Erin's video.
- 1 Erin is alone and bored.
- 3 Erin follows Griff and Nell up the hill.
- 5 Erin decides to film it all.
- 4 They watch Nell with the sheep far down in the valley.

Du muss nicht jedes Wort in einem Text verstehen. Um ein schnellen Überblick über den Inhalt zu bekommen, überfliegst du den Text.

b)

1 grandparents
2 enjoy
3 Nell and the sheep
4 ridge; valley
5 moves the sheep
6 shakes his head
7 shows them the/her video

3 Words Digital grandma

Beth	OK, first you need to (1) **charge** your tablet so that it has power.
Grandma	Yes, I've done that already. What does this button mean?
Beth	That's where you (2) **switch on** your tablet.
Grandma	Oh! There – now it's on. How nice! But where's the internet?
Beth	Oh, Grandma! You have to (3) **connect** your tablet to Wi-Fi first.
Grandma	Well, how should I know that? Oh look, it's telling me to (4) **set up** all these things – language, password, email, ... That sounds like a lot of work.
Beth	It's not that bad. You can do it later. You just (5) **tap** on these icons.
Grandma	OK. And your mum wants me to (6) **install** a social media app called Buzz so that I can (7) **post** photos and things like the rest of you.
Beth	Then I should also show you how to (8) **edit** your photos so that they look nice.
Grandma	My photos always look nice, sweetheart. What's this? Does this mean I can (9) **swipe** through my photos like on a phone?
Beth	Exactly. You don't need my help, Grandma. You're already a digital granny!

4 Language It can happen in Wales

1 'We**'re/are going to miss** the train!'
2 They**'re/are going to set up** their tent.
3 It**'s/is going to rain**.
4 She**'s/is going to go** surfing.
5 The water **is going to hit** her.
6 He**'s/is going to order** a burger.
7 She**'s/is going to post** a photo.
8 They**'re/are going to watch** a rugby match.

5 Language Talking about social media

1 which
2 who
3 which
4 which
5 who
6 who

!

Mit Relativsätzen kannst du zusätzliche Informationen über eine Person oder eine Sache geben. Sie werden in der Regel durch Relativpronomen *who*, *which* oder *that* eingeleitet:

- Für Personen, verwendest du *who*.
- Für Dinge, benutzt du *which*.
- Das Relativpronomen *that* kann für Personen oder Dinge stehen.

6 Language Crazy about cosplay

1 yours
2 mine
3 Hers
4 yours
5 theirs
6 his
7 ours

!

mit Nomen	ohne Nomen
my friend	mine
your friend	yours
his / her / its friend	his / hers / its
our friend	ours
your friend	yours
their friend	theirs

7 MEDIATION Gaming console instructions

(Lösungsbeispiel)

1 Bitte ein Elternteil die Play-1-Website aufzurufen und ein Play-1-Konto für dich einzurichten.
2 Schalte deine Spielkonsole ein.
3 Tippe im Hauptmenü auf „Manage your account“ (Verwalten Sie Ihr Konto).
4 Verknüpfe dein Play-1-Konto mit deiner Spielkonsole.
5 Gehe zurück zum Hauptmenü. Tippe auf „Play-1 E-Shop“. Dadurch gelangst du zum Online-Shop, in dem du aus Hunderten von Spielen auswählen kannst.
6 Wähle ein Spiel und tippe auf „Buy“ (Kaufen).
7 Warte, bis ein „Thank you“-Fenster (Danke-Fenster) erscheint. Dann erscheint ein weiteres Fenster mit einer grünen Schaltfläche „Download“ (Herunterladen). Tippe auf die Schaltfläche und lade dein neues Spiel herunter.

8 WRITING A difficult question

Benutze die Checkliste um zu kontrollieren, ob du die Aufgabe erfüllt hast.

Did you ...		
include three good aspects of social media?	connect / stay in touch with friends and family • find information • find people with the same interests and hobbies • have fun • learn new things • use creativity	*2 Punkte pro Aspekt = 6 Punkte* ______/ 6
include three bad things about social media?	spend all day looking at screens • cyberbullying • feel bad about yourself in comparison • feel like you're missing out on things • get fake information • lose sleep • lose touch with the real world • no time for other things	*2 Punkte pro Aspekt = 6 Punkte* ______/ 6
give your opinion?	I believe ... • I think ... • I would say that ... • If you ask me, ... • In my opinion, ...	______/ 3
		Total: ______/ 15

(Lösungsbeispiel)

Hi Malia,

Here's what I think: Social media has good and bad sides.

First some of the good things: It's great for staying in touch with friends and family. You can learn a lot of cool things on social media. And you can show your creativity by posting artwork or sharing hobbies.

Some of the bad things are: Too much screen time is not healthy. Seeing other people's posts about fun things they're doing can make you feel like you're missing something. And some people use social media to say mean things or bully others.

Malia, I would say that you need to decide what is most important to you. The choice is yours!

Bye,

Murat

9 WORDS A message home

1 voice • **2** breaking up • **3** stay in touch • **4** ship • **5** roller coaster • **6** donkeys • **7** waterfall • **8** versus • **9** national • **10** actually

Speaking

1 Ireland and the United Kingdom

05

(Lösungsbeispiel)

a)

I'll start with photo A. In the middle of the photo there's the Tower Bridge in London. On the left you can see a ship and some boats on the river. In the background there are some skyscrapers. At the bottom of the photo you can see buses and cars crossing the bridge.

Photo B shows a place in Ireland. It's a sunny day and there are colourful little houses in the foreground. There's an old church on the right – it's much bigger than the houses. I can see some water in the background.

In the middle of photo C there's a river. In the foreground there's a small waterfall and in the background there are more waterfalls and a small bridge. The Brecon Beacons in Wales look like an amazing place.

Photo D is a picture of Scotland. There's an old castle in the foreground. At the bottom of the picture you can see some old ruins from the castle. In the middle and in the background there's a great view of Loch Ness. And if you look closely, you can see Nessie swimming around! Just joking!

Alle Lösungsbeispiele aus diesem Kapitel kannst du aus deiner Cornelsen Lernen App abspielen.

b)

Now I'd like to answer question B. The UK is a group of four countries: England, Wales, Scotland and Northern Ireland. Ireland is an island with two countries: the Republic of Ireland and Northern Ireland. The Republic of Ireland is much bigger than Northern Ireland. It's part of the EU. Northern Ireland is not. It's part of the UK.

2 A cool outfit

06

(Lösungsbeispiel)

a)

I often wear baggy trousers, a colourful T-shirt, sunglasses and a crazy hat. I like this outfit because it's fun and comfortable. When I wear it I feel confident. I think attractive and trendy clothes make me feel more confident because they say more about me. I also feel confident when I play sports and when I'm with my mum and dad. They make me feel confident because I know they believe in me.

Schaue dein Publikum an und warte, bis es ruhig ist. Sprich langsam, laut und deutlich.

b)

The outfit in photo A looks a bit trendier than my outfit. The jeans are tighter than mine and the sweatshirt is a trendy colour. But the trainers aren't as nice as my trainers. And I don't like the sunglasses. My sunglasses came from a second-hand shop and I think they're more interesting than the ones in the picture.

07

3 Social media

(Lösungsbeispiel)

a)

To answer the first question, yes. I use social media because I think it's a great way to stay in touch with my friends and family.

b)

I'm quite active – I use it nearly every day. I always check my messages and see what other people are posting. I like to post messages and I sometimes upload photos. I often chat with my friends too.

c)

Now for part C. First I'll talk about the arguments against social media. One of the problems is that there's a lot of cyberbullying. I've spoken to kids at my own school who have experienced bullying online. Another problem is that teens think they need to get likes on social media before they can feel good about themselves. I think that's sad. And a third problem is that a lot of people post photos that they have edited, so they look much better than in real life. It's really stupid and it makes other kids feel bad about themselves.
Now for some arguments for social media. Social media can be good for teens because they can have more contact with friends and family and that can make them feel good. Also, social media is a good way to get news and other information. And finally, you can be very creative with social media, so it's a good way to try different things and learn new skills online.

08

4 In a restaurant

(Lösungsbeispiel)

Partner A Hi, are you ready to order?
Partner B Yes, I am.
Partner A What would you like to drink?
Partner B I'd like sparkling water, please.
Partner A OK. And to eat?
Partner B I'll have fish and chips.
Partner A Sure.
Partner B Could I have a small green salad with that, please?
Partner A Yes, no problem. Anything else?
Partner B No, that's all. Thank you.

Let's talk (Schulbuch, S. 207–214) enthält Wendungen für wichtige Situationen, wie z. B.: Essen gehen und in einem Restaurant bestellen.

09

5 Interests and adventures

(Lösungsbeispiel)

Partner A Have you ever gone windsurfing?
Partner B No, I haven't.
Partner A What about paddleboarding? Have you tried that?
Partner B I haven't tried that yet, but I've tried kayaking.
Partner A Cool! What was it like?
Partner B It was a lot of fun. I was with my brother in a kayak and the river was strong, so we went really fast. What about you? What have you tried?
Partner A I've been in a small boat too, but we didn't go kayaking. We went fishing.
Partner B Oh wow. Did you catch a fish?
Partner A No, I didn't. But it was still fun. After that we went swimming in the sea. That was cool. Have you ever swum in the sea?
Partner B Yes, I have. I also jumped from a cliff into the water. Have you ever tried cliff jumping?
Partner A No, I haven't. That's too scary for me.

10

6 Exercise At a B&B

(Lösungsbeispiel)

Dialogue 1

Partner A Hello, Blarney B&B, can I help you?
Partner B Hi, I'd like to book a room, but first I have some questions.
Partner A Yes, sure.
Partner B How much are your rooms?
Partner A All our rooms are €80 per night.
Partner B We'd like a room with twin beds. Is that possible?
Partner A Yes, that's no problem.
Partner B Great. And does the room have its own bathroom?
Partner A Yes. All our rooms have a private bathroom.
Partner B Oh good. Do you have Wi-Fi?
Partner A Yes, our rooms have both Wi-Fi and TV.
Partner B Great. I'm vegetarian. Do you offer a vegetarian breakfast?
Partner A Yes, we do.
Partner B How much does the breakfast cost?
Partner A That's included in the price of your room.
Partner B Super. Is it possible to have a tea or coffee in our room?
Partner A Yes, your room will have a kettle, so you can make your own warm drinks.
Partner B One last thing: Is there a place nearby where we can hire bikes?
Partner A You can get them right here! Guests can borrow our bikes for free.
Partner B Perfect! Then I'd like to book a room.

!

Füllworter
Um ein Gespräch nicht stocken zu lassen, kannst du Füllwörter verwenden. Wenn du Zeit zum Nachdenken brauchst, kannst du diese mit *Let me see ..., Just a minute,* oder *Well, ...* überbrücken.

Dialogue 2

Partner B Cliffs of Erin B&B, good afternoon.
Partner A Hello, I'd like to book a room, but first I have a few questions.
Partner B No problem.
Partner A How much do your rooms cost?
Partner B The price starts at £85 per night.
Partner A We'd like a room with a double bed. How much is that?
Partner B That costs a bit more, £150.
Partner A OK. And do your rooms have private bathrooms?
Partner B Some of them do. That costs £200 per night.
Partner A Oh! Well, does the room have a TV?
Partner B Yes, our rooms have both Wi-Fi and TV.
Partner A Great. Do you offer a cooked breakfast?
Partner B Yes, we have a breakfast buffet. It costs ... let me see ... £15 per day.
Partner A Um, alright. Is there a kettle in the room? And does it cost extra?
Partner B We have a kettle for tea and coffee in our living room downstairs. We have books and games too.
Partner A Well, we like games. What about dogs? Are dogs allowed?
Partner B Yes, dogs are welcome! And we have two very nice dogs who live here.
Partner A Oh, no. That's it. I'm allergic to dogs. I think I'll look for a different B&B. Thank you for your time.
Partner B Happy to help! Have a nice day!

Unit 5 Two Irelands: Together

1 LISTENING I'm here!

11

Hörtext

Fionn Hi Oona! How's my favourite cousin?
Oona Hi Fionn! I'm great and I'm finally here! We arrived last night.
Fionn Nice! How was the trip?
Oona It was long. We left Limerick at one and we got here at about 7:30 in the evening.
Fionn Wow. That's six and a half hours.
Oona But it was OK, actually. Our team is a lot of fun. And when you take the train you see amazing landscapes that you don't see from a car or a bus.
Fionn I know what you mean.
Oona It's interesting, too, how some things look different here in Northern Ireland, like the road signs.
Fionn Yeah. You're in the UK now! So where are you staying?
Oona We're in a little B&B.
Fionn Cool! Do you know what part of Belfast you're in?
Oona Someone told me we're in Ardoyne. Is that a nice part of town?
Fionn It is, actually, and it's not far from our house. Do you have your own room in your B&B?
Oona No, I'm sharing with my friend Lucy. It's fun. We have a room with twin beds.
Fionn Do you have your own bathroom?
Oona Yes, we do. But the shower is down the hall.
Fionn Oh. That's not so great.
Oona It's fine. We only stay here for two days, so I don't mind.
Fionn I once stayed in a B&B in Dublin. I remember our room had a kettle, so we could make tea. That was cool. Does yours have one?
Oona No. They took the kettle out of our room because it doesn't work.
Fionn Oh. Well, I'm sure it's still a nice room.
Oona It is! There's a TV if we want to watch something, and, most importantly, there's wi-fi, so I think we're OK.
Fionn That's good. And you can have tea with breakfast, right?
Oona Yes! We had an amazing cooked breakfast in the dining room. I'm so full.
Fionn When are we going to see each other, Oona? I can't wait!
Oona Are you going to come to the competition?
Fionn I can't come this morning, but I'd like to come in the afternoon. Do you know what time you perform?
Oona No, the judges haven't told us yet. I'll let you know when we find out.
Fionn OK. And can you text me the school address too?
Oona Yes, sure.
Fionn Do you think that you'll win?
Oona I don't know. I think we can beat the other teams, but our aim right now is just to do well.
Fionn I'm cheering for you. Good luck!
Oona Thanks. See you later!

a)

Transport:

Accommodation:

Oona and Lucy have...

	Yes	No
a double bed.		✓
twin beds.	✓	
their own bathroom.	✓	
their own shower.		✓
a kettle.		✓
Wi-Fi.	✓	
a TV.	✓	
a cooked breakfast.	✓	

b)

1 b) • **2** c) • **3** a) • **4** b) • **5** a) • **6** c)

2 READING Life in Belfast

a)

1 Victoria Square
2 St George's Market
3 Grand Opera House
4 Windsor Park
5 Shankill Road

b)

1 recommended; tours
2 cycled; expensive
3 history; stand
4 worker; pitch
5 photographed; rain
6 allowed; brother

3 WORDS Trip to Northern Ireland

1 time • **2** abroad • **3** ID card • **4** B&B • **5** recommended • **6** cab • **7** divides • **8** Catholic • **9** the Troubles • **10** construction • **11** spectacular • **12** confused

Wie merke ich mir neue Wörter besser?
Manchmal macht es Sinn ***phrases*** statt Einzelwörter zu lernen. ***Phrases*** sind Ausdrücke, die aus mehreren Wörtern bestehen, z. B. *a bottle of water = eine Flasche Wasser*. Lerne alo nicht *bottle* und *water* als Einzelwörter, sondern den ganzen Ausdruck: *a bottle of water*.

4 Mediation At a B&B

(Lösungsbeispiel)

1 She would like to know the difference between twin beds and double beds.
2 Er sagt, dass twin beds zwei Einzelbetten sind. Einige Zimmer haben ein Doppelbett, aber leider sind die im Moment alle ausgebucht.
3 She says that a room with twin beds is perfect.
4 Er möchte, dass Sie dieses Formular ausfüllen. Und er möchte ihre Reisepässe sehen.
5 How much is breakfast?
6 Er sagt, ein warmes Frühstück ist im Preis inklusive.
7 How much is the room?
8 Er sagt, alle Zimmer kosten 80 Pfund.

Keine Panik vor unbekannten Wörtern
Wenn du für jemanden vermitteln möchtest, musst du nicht alle Details übersetzen. Deshalb ist es auch in Ordnung, wenn du nicht jedes Wort, sondern nur die zentrale Aussage verstehst. Wenn du ein Wort nicht kennst, versuche es mit anderen Wörtern zu umschreiben.

5 Writing The big day

Benutze die Checkliste um zu kontrollieren, ob du die Aufgabe erfüllt hast. Gib dir drei Punkte für jede Frage, die du mit „ja" beantwortest. Wenn du die Aufgabe nur zum Teil erfüllt hast, gib dir zwei Punkte.

Did you ...		✓
use the simple past?	practised • took • travelled • were • got • ...	
describe what happens in all six pictures?		
use at least 3 linking words?	and • but • so • finally • ...	
use at least 3 time phrases?	every day • later • after that • then • ...	
write at least 70 words?		
	Total: ______ / 15	

(Lösungsbeispiel)
Every day Sophie practised her routine for the dance competition at home. On the big day she and her dad took the bus, but the bus travelled very slowly and they were worried. When they finally got off the bus, they had to hurry to the competition. They arrived late and the woman at the door was not happy. Finally, Sophie's big moment came. She was nervous. Everyone watched as she performed her routine on stage. Later, the judges announced the winner. Sophie was surprised when she won. It was an amazing day.

6 Words Writing home

1 accommodation
2 twin beds
3 kettle
4 cooked breakfast
5 buffet
6 cereals
7 cold meats
8 form
9 passport
10 guests

Wie merke ich mir neue Wörter besser?
Beim Vokabeln lernen kann es hilfreich sein, wenn du gegensätzliche Wörter und Wörter mit der gleichen Bedeutung sammelst.

Unit 4
Wales: Digital life

04

1 LISTENING How are things? _____ / 9

▸ SB, pp. 114–115, p. 175

a) **Alfie has posted some photos on his social media page. Look at them carefully. Then listen to his phone conversation with his friend Beth. Tick (✓) the photos that he wants to delete.** *(3 points)*

A

A great rugby match!

B

These guys are everywhere!

C

Beach day near Swansea!

D

Conwy Castle is so cool!

E

Beauty in the Brecon Beacons

F

I love this little lighthouse!

b) **Listen again to Alfie and Beth. Circle the correct answer – a), b) or c).** *(6 points)*

1 The photos that Alfie posted ...
   a) haven't got any likes.
   b) have got a few likes.
   c) have got a lot of likes.

2 Beth is surprised that Alfie didn't ...
   a) have a great time in Wales.
   b) like the lighthouse.
   c) go to the lighthouse.

3 Alfie went hiking ...
   a) and saw some sheep.
   b) but didn't see any sheep.
   c) but didn't take any photos.

4 When people talk to Alfie about his photos ...
   a) he doesn't want to lie to them.
   b) he knows he had an amazing holiday.
   c) he's happy that he posted them.

5 Beth is jealous that Alfie ...
   a) saw lots of cute sheep.
   b) went to Conwy Castle.
   c) went to a rugby match.

6 Alfie knows that he needs to stop ...
   a) deleting his holiday photos.
   b) worrying about what other people think.
   c) posting on social media.

▸ Check

2 Reading In a Welsh village ______ / 15

▶ SB, pp. 120–122, p. 176

Erin was bored. Her dad and brother were at a shopping centre in Chester. Her mum and Aunt Dilys were busy with old boxes. The quiet, old house smelled of Erin's grandparents, who she still missed. Erin put on her rain jacket and went for a walk.

The green hills behind the village seemed to grow higher under the grey clouds. Erin spotted some flowers and took a photo with her phone.

'It's better just to enjoy them. A photo's never the same,' a voice said.

She looked up and saw old Griff, her grandpa's brother, coming out of his farmhouse. He smiled. 'You kids and your devices.'

Erin smiled back but didn't know what to say.

He waved with his walking stick, then called his dog, Nell, and turned onto a path that went up into the hills.

'Where are you going, Griff?' Erin asked.

'To check on the sheep,' he said.

Erin looked around. 'But where are they?'

'Come along! We'll show you,' he said.

Erin was curious, so she followed.

They walked slowly and Erin asked Griff questions about Nell and the sheep. Nell ran far up the hill and didn't come back.

'Erm, she's gone,' Erin said.

Griff walked on without looking up. 'She knows where to go,' he said with a laugh.

At the top of the hill they stood on the ridge and looked far down into the next valley.

'There,' he said, pointing with his walking stick.

Erin heard sheep and then a dog barking far away. Then she saw them, little white spots that moved together over the green hills. A black spot was close behind them. Griff shouted a word in Welsh and the dog stopped, looked, then ran to catch two sheep.

Amazing, Erin thought.

'Could I film this?' she asked.

Griff's attention was on the sheep. 'If you like.'

They watched Nell slowly move the sheep up the hill towards them. Erin filmed it all. She also filmed Griff watching the sheep, calling to Nell.

'She's so smart!' Erin said.

Griff laughed. 'She sure makes my life easier!'

After an hour they left the sheep and walked slowly back down to the village. The sun came out. Nell ran in front of them and Erin stopped a few times to film. Griff saw this and shook his head.

At the farmhouse Griff's wife Trina made tea. Erin had more questions about the sheep farm. Griff answered and shook his head as Erin filmed.

Later that evening after dinner, Erin tapped the editing app, uploaded all the videos and began cutting the parts she didn't need. She added some soft guitar music, captions and a title. Then she checked the edited video and finally felt happy with it.

The next day Erin went up the hill again with Griff and Nell. This time Trina came along. On the ridge they had a rest and Erin showed them the video. It was called *A good life*. When it was over, Griff was quiet. His eyes were wet as he kept looking at the screen.

'Maybe those devices aren't so bad,' he said.

a) **Read the story. Then number the events in the right order.** *(7 points)*

- ☐ They drink tea and talk about the sheep farm.
- ☐ Erin photographs some flowers.
- ☐ Griff becomes quiet when he sees Erin's video.
- ☐ Erin is alone and bored.
- ☐ Erin follows Griff and Nell up the hill.
- ☐ Erin decides to film it all.
- ☐ They watch Nell with the sheep far down in the valley.

▶ Check

b) **Read again and complete the sentences.** *(8 points)*

1 Erin misses her ______________________________.

2 Griff tells Erin just to ______________________________ the flowers.

3 As they walk up the hill, Erin and Griff talk about ______________________________.

4 Standing up on the ____________________, they look down into the ____________________.

5 Erin films the scene as Nell ______________________________ up the hill towards them.

6 When Griff sees Erin filming, he ______________________________.

7 When Erin goes up the hill with them the next day, she ______________________________.

3 WORDS Digital grandma ____ /9

▸ SB, pp. 122–123, p. 206

Beth's grandma has bought a tablet and needs Beth's help. Complete their dialogue with the words in the box. There is one more word than you need.

charge • connect • edit • install • post • set up • swipe • switch on • tap • terms

Beth OK, first you need to (1) ______________ your tablet so that it has power.

Grandma Yes, I've done that already. What does this button mean?

Beth That's where you (2) ______________ your tablet.

Grandma Oh! There – now it's on. How nice! But where's the internet?

Beth Oh, Grandma! You have to (3) ______________ your tablet to Wi-Fi first.

Grandma Well, how should I know that? Oh look, it's telling me to (4) ______________ all these things – language, password, email, ... That sounds like a lot of work.

Beth It's not that bad. You can do it later. You just (5) ______________ on these icons.

Grandma OK. And your mum wants me to (6) ______________ a social media app called Buzz so that I can (7) ______________ photos and things like the rest of you.

Beth Then I should also show you how to (8) ______________ your photos so that they look nice.

Grandma My photos always look nice, sweetheart. What's this? Does this mean I can (9) ______________ through my photos like on a phone?

Beth Exactly. You don't need my help, Grandma. You're already a digital granny!

▸ Check

Erklär-film

4 Language It can happen in Wales ____ /8

► SB, p. 121, p. 145, p. 194

Look at the situations in the pictures. Write what you think is going to happen. Use the going to-future and a verb from the box.

1

2

3

4

5

6

7

8

go • hit • miss • order • post • rain • set up • watch

!

Mit *going to* ... sagst du, was du vorhast oder planst. Du kannst auch sagen, was wahrscheinlich passieren wird. Das *going to-future* besteht aus drei Teilen: Form von *be* + *going to* + Verb.

I'm going to visit Wales this summer. My sister is going to come too. We're going to have a lot of fun!

1 'We ______________________ the train!'

2 They ______________________ their tent.

3 It ______________________.

4 She ______________________ surfing.

5 The water ______________________ her.

6 He ______________________ a burger.

7 She ______________________ a photo.

8 They ______________________ a rugby match.

► Check

Erklär-film

5 LANGUAGE Talking about social media ____ /6

►SB, pp. 126–127, p. 147, p. 195

Read these students' statements about social media. Complete them with *who* or *which*.

1 Some kids say things online ______________ are really mean.

2 I think people ______________ don't try to stop cyberbullying are part of the problem.

3 Before you post a photo ______________ shows other people, you should ask them.

4 I prefer social networks ______________ do more to protect their users.

5 I know two students in my class ______________ have deleted their social media apps.

6 Jo Martin is an influencer ______________ I like to follow because he's a really funny guy.

6 LANGUAGE Crazy about cosplay ____ /7

►SB, p. 116, p. 193

A group of friends are getting excited about their cosplay competition. Read and complete their text messages with the correct possessive pronouns from the box.

mine • yours (2x) • hers • his • ours • theirs

Hey cosplayers! My costume is going to be so cool. What about (1) ______________ ?

Hari, your costumes are always cool. But I'm learning from you. When you see (2) ______________ , you'll be jealous for sure.

I don't think my costume will have a chance against Megan's. (3) ______________ looks exactly like the main character's costume in the series Waterfall Soldier. Amazing!

Yeah, Megan's costume is awesome, but I think (4) ______________ looks great too, Sunya. You put so much work into your Silver Wizard.

Ben and Yuri are going to be goblin fighters. Their costumes look amazing. I think they got some help with (5) ______________ from Ben's mum.

I remember Yuri had one of the best ogre costumes last year. (6) ______________ was nearly as good as Hari's.

When we all went to that comic book event last summer, we saw a lot of great costumes, but I thought (7) ______________ were the best. I think we can be proud, guys!

►Check

7 MEDIATION Gaming console instructions ___ / 7

► SB, pp. 122–123, p. 177, p. 206

Your little sister wants to download a game onto her new Play-1 gaming console. She finds some instructions, but they're in English only. Help her and explain steps 1 through 7 in German.

1 Ask a parent to go to the Play-1 website and set up a Play-1 account for you.
2 Switch on your gaming console.
3 In the main menu, tap on 'Manage your account'.
4 Link your Play-1 account with your gaming console.
5 Go back to the main menu. Tap on 'Play-1 E-Shop'. This takes you to our online shop where you can choose from hundreds of games.
6 Choose a game and tap on 'buy'.
7 Wait for a 'Thank you' window to appear. Then another window will appear with a green 'Download' button. Tap the button and download your new game.

Bei einer Mediation-Aufgabe gibst du normalerweise nur den wesentlichen Inhalt wieder. Nur bei Gebrauchsanweisungen ist es wichtig, genau zu sein.

1 ______________________________

____

2 ______________________________

____

3 ______________________________

____

4 ______________________________

____

5 ______________________________

____

6 ______________________________

____

7 ______________________________

____

► Check

8 WRITING **A difficult question** _____ / 15

▶ More help, p. 76 ▶ SB, pp. 124–127, p. 172, p.180

You're emailing with your friend Malia. She's thinking about deleting her social media account after some negative experiences. Write an email and give your opinion. Include three good things and three bad things about social media and give reasons. Use opinion phrases. Write 80 words or more.

You can use the pictures for help. Use your own ideas too.

Good:

Bad:

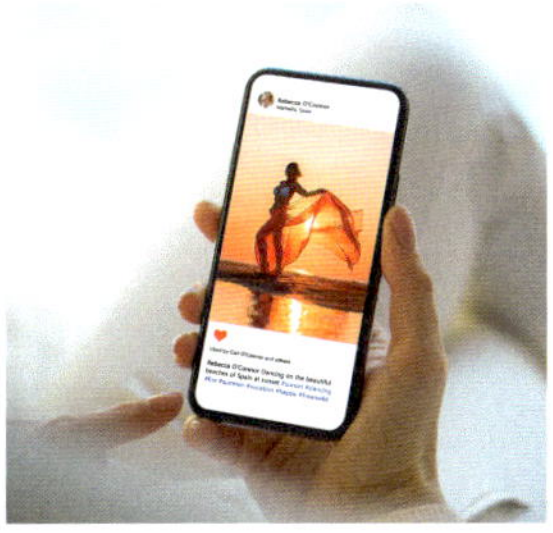

You can start like this:

Hi Malia,

Here's what I think: ____________________

▶ Check

9 WORDS A message home ______ / 10

► SB, pp. 249–258

Ryan is on an exchange in Wales. He wants to contact his mum, but he's tired of texting, so he's trying something different. Complete his message to his mum with the words in the box. There are two more words than you need.

actually • breaking up • diary • donkeys • mining • national • roller coaster • ship • stay in touch • versus • voice • waterfall

'Hi Mum. I agree with you now that (1) ______________ messages are easier. When I called you a few days ago, I couldn't hear you well. You kept (2) ______________. So maybe this is a better way to (3) ______________. I'm doing fine. We've done some cool things. We visited a harbour where they're building a really big (4) ______________. After that we went to a theme park and rode the (5) ______________. I wasn't scared at all! We also visited a farm that had (6) ______________ and I rode one. It wasn't like riding a horse. The farm was in a valley with a big (7) ______________. Oh, and last night we watched a rugby match on TV. Can you believe it? It was Wales (8) ______________ Ireland. Their (9) ______________ team isn't as strong as ours, but it was a close game, (10) ______________. Wales nearly won. But rugby is boring for you, Mum, I know, so I'll stop now. Lots of love! Bye!'

Bereich	Aufgabe	erreichte Punktzahl	🤩	😎	🤔	😭
listening	1	______ / 9	9	8–7	6–5	4–0
reading	2	______ / 15	15–14	13–11	10–8	7–0
words	3 9	______ / 9 ______ / 10 } ______ /19	19–17	16–13	12–10	9–0
language	4 5 6	______ / 8 ______ / 6 ______ / 7 } ______ /21	21–19	18–15	14–11	10–0
mediation	7	______ / 7	7	6–5	4	3–0
writing	8	______ / 15	15–14	13–11	10–8	7–0
Gesamt		______ / 86	86–78	77–60	59–43	42–0

► Check

Speaking

1 Monologue Ireland and the United Kingdom (Hello, Unit 1) ► SB, pp. 10–13, pp. 14–15, p. 178

05

a) Look at the four pictures. What can you see? Make notes.

A

London, England

B

County Cork, Ireland

C

Brecon Beacons, Wales

D

Loch Ness, Scotland

Now describe the pictures. You can use the phrases in the box below and your own ideas.

> I'll start with photo A. • At the top/bottom of the photo ... • In the background/foreground ... • In the middle of photo B, there's ... • Now I'll talk about photo C. • On the right/left (of photo A) you can see ... • Photo D shows ...

b) What do you know about the United Kingdom and Ireland? Which countries are part of the UK? How are Northern Ireland and the Republic of Ireland different?

Höre dir die Lösungsbeispiele an und achte nicht nur auf den Inhalt, sondern auch auf Aussprache und Intonation.

► Check

2 MONOLOGUE A cool outfit (Unit 2)

06

▸ SB, p. 50, p. 52, pp. 58–61, p. 187, p. 200

a) **Think of an outfit that you often wear. Make notes about the outfit and answer these questions:**

- Describe your outfit.
- How do you feel when you wear this outfit?
- Do clothes make you feel confident?
- What (other) things/people make you feel confident and why?

I often like to wear tight trousers with a colourful sweatshirt and …

I think clothes make me feel confident because …

Now talk about your outfit and about feeling confident.

b) **Compare your outfit with the outfit in photo A or photo B. How are they similar? How are they different? You can use the words and phrases in the boxes and your own ideas:**

attractive • baggy • boring • cheap • colourful • cool • crazy • fun • interesting • nice • old-fashioned • patterned • plain • sporty • tight • trendy	blazer • boots • dress • glasses • hat • hoodie • jacket • jeans • jewellry • scarf • shoes • shorts • skirt • socks • sunglasses • sweatshirt • trainers • trousers • T-shirt

I think the outfit in photo A/B is The trousers in the photo are	tighter than trendier than more old-fashioned than	my outfit. my trousers. my trainers. mine.
The outfit in the photo isn't The trainers in the photo aren't	as cool as as crazy as as interesting as	
I like the outfit in the photo I don't like the T-shirt in the photo I like my sunglasses	because it looks because they look	boring. fun. plain.

Nimm dich beim Üben auf. Danach kannst du kontrollieren, ob du wirklich alles gesagt hast, was du sagen wolltest.

▸ Check

3 Monologue Social media (Unit 4)

07

▸ SB, pp. 124–127, pp. 132–133, p. 211

Talk about social media. Think first about the following questions, organize your thoughts and make notes. You can use the phrases in the boxes and your own ideas.

a) Do you use social media? Why (not)?

I (don't) use social media because … • I (don't) think it's … • I (don't) like/need/want to use it because … • It's bad/good for …

b) If you use social media, how active are you? What do you use it for?

chat with friends • check my messages • get information • post photos and videos • read and watch the news • see what other people are posting • send messages

c) What are at some arguments for and against social media? Talk about three good things and three bad things. You can use the pictures and phrases in the boxes below.

Social media is good/bad for teens because … • It's a good way to … • Social media helps people … • One of the problems with social media is that … • Another problem is that …

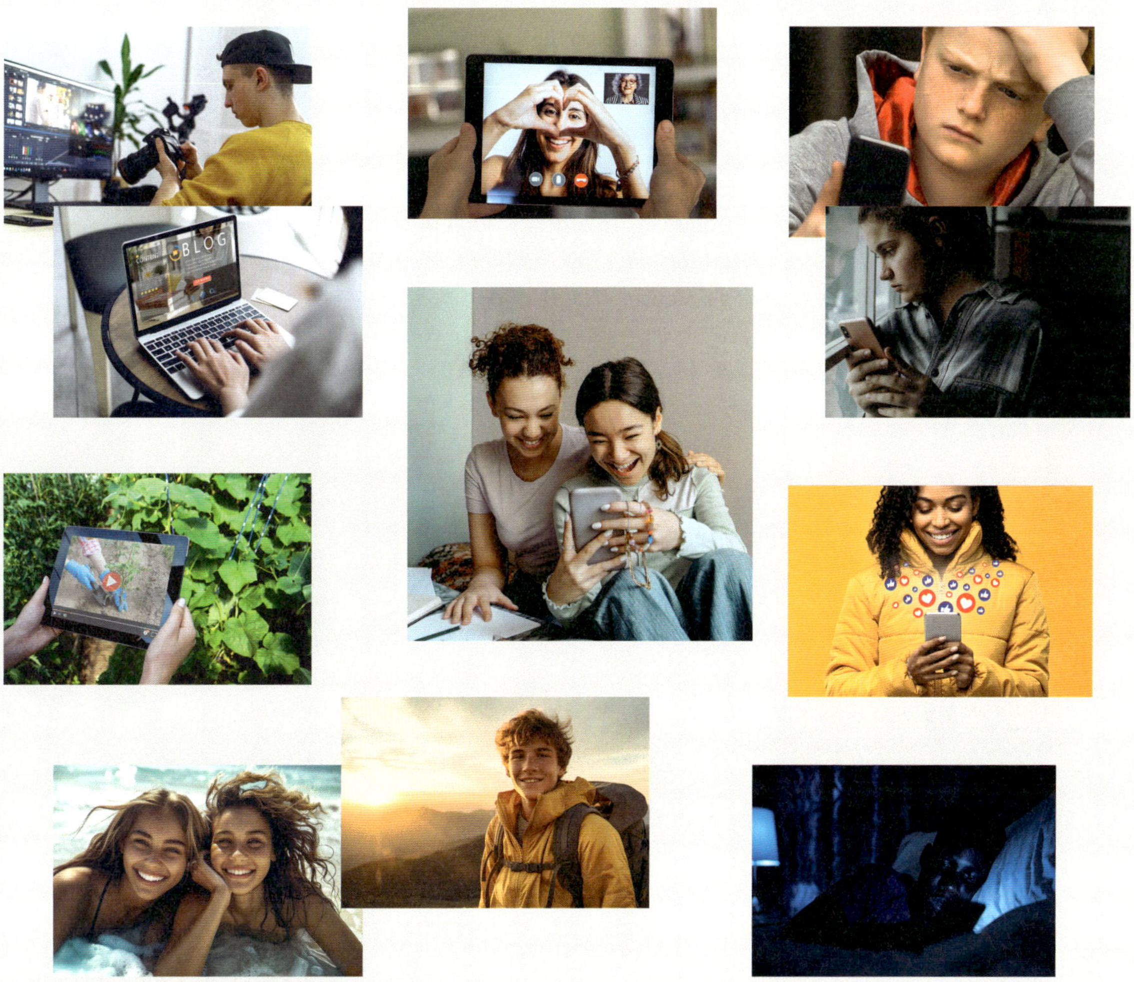

▸ Check

4 DIALOGUE In a restaurant (Unit 1)

08

▸SB, p. 26, p. 209

a) You are in a restaurant. Partner A is the waiter.
Partner B orders food and drinks from the menu below.
You can use the phrases in the box and your own ideas.

Menu

FOOD

Chicken curry	£9.25	Fish and chips	£9.75
Lamb kebab	£9.50	Potato and broccoli curry	£8.50
Beef burger	£9.50	Avocado and tomato salad	£6.50
Veggie burger	£8.75	Green salad	small £3.75 large £5.75

DRINKS

Tap water	free	Lemonade	£2.90	Tea	£2.00
Sparkling water	£2.50	Milkshake	£4.60	Coffee	£2.30

Waiter: Are you ready to order? • What would you like (to eat/drink)? • Anything else? • No problem. • Sure. • OK, thank you.
Customer: Yes, please. • I'd like ..., please. • Could I have ...? • I'll have ... • Can I have it with/without ...? • Can you tell me what is in the ...?

You can start like this:

Partner A *Hi, are you ready to order?*

Partner B *Yes, I am.*

Partner A *What would you like to drink?*

Partner B *I'd like ..., please.*

Partner A *Right. And to eat?*

...

b) Swap roles and do the role play again.

Wenn du Dialoge übst, finde ein Gegenüber, mit dem du zusammen üben kannst, am besten jemand aus deinem Englischkurs. Du kannst auch eine Freundin, einen Freund, oder jemand in deiner Familie, der Englisch spricht, bitten, mit dir Dialoge zu üben.

▸Check

09

5 Dialogue **Interests and adventures (Unit 3)**

► SB, pp. 86–89, pp. 192–193, p. 203

You and your partner are watching a friend who is trying windsurfing for the first time. You start talking about interesting and adventurous outdoor activities. Find out what your partner has already done and what it was like. You can use ideas from the pictures and from the box or you can use your own ideas.

climb a tree • go kayaking • go on a long bike tour • hike in the mountains • ride a horse • swim in a river • sleep under the stars • watch a sunrise or sunset

You can start like this:

Partner A *Have you ever …?*

Partner B *No, I haven't.*

Partner A *What about …? Have you tried that?*

Partner B *I haven't tried that yet, but I've tried …*

Partner A *Cool! What was that like?*

Partner B *It was …*

Fehlt dir beim Sprechen ein Wort oder fällt es dir nicht ein, kannst du es umschreiben, z. B. durch einen Oberbegriff (*umbrella word*), mit Wörtern, die eine ähnliche oder gleiche Bedeutung haben, oder mit gegensätzlichen Wörtern. Auch mit Relativsätzen kannst du Eigenschaften des gesuchten Begriffes erklären.

It's a sport that's very similar to …

► Check

6 DIALOGUE At a B&B (Unit 5)

10

► SB, p. 151, p. 153, p. 260

Work with a partner and agree on your roles – Partner A or Partner B. Then look at your role cards. Partner A starts. When you are finished, do the second role play. Then partner B starts.

Partner A

Dialogue 1

You work at The Blarney B&B. Partner B calls with some questions. Look at the information in the description below.
Then answer Partner B's questions.

The Blarney B&B
Welcome to The Blarney B&B, your Irish home away from home in County Kerry, Ireland! Our family-run B&B offers double and twin rooms for €80 per night, all with their own bathrooms, Wi-Fi and TV. Each room comes with a kettle for your morning tea. Enjoy a full cooked breakfast included in the price, with vegetarian alternatives. And guests can borrow our bikes and scooters for free. Enjoy the beauty of Ireland at The Blarney B&B. Book your stay with us today!

Dialogue 2

You want to book a room in a B&B. A friend recommends Cliffs of Erin B&B to you, so you call the B&B with some questions.
Ask Partner B questions about ...

1 *price*
2 *room with double bed*
3 *private bathroom*
4 *TV*
5 *cooked breakfast*
6 *kettle in the room*
7 *dogs allowed?*

Partner B

Dialogue 1

You're going to Ireland and want to book a room in a B&B. Someone recommends The Blarney B&B to you, so you call the B&B with some questions. Ask Partner A questions about ...

1 *price*
2 *room with twin beds*
3 *own bathroom*
4 *Wi-Fi*
5 *vegetarian breakfast*
6 *kettle in the room*
7 *bikes and bike tours*

Dialogue 2

You work at Cliffs of Erin B&B. Partner A calls with some questions. Look at the information in the description below.
Then answer Partner A's questions.

Cliffs of Erin B&B
Welcome to Cliffs of Erin B&B, your home in the beautiful landscapes of Northern Ireland! Our comfortable rooms, starting from £85 per night, offer double or twin beds, some with private bathrooms. All of our rooms have Wi-Fi and TV. Enjoy our breakfast buffet and relax in our living room with books, games and a kettle for tea and coffee. Dogs are welcome! Book your Northern Ireland holiday today at Cliffs of Erin B&B!

► Check

Unit 5
Two Irelands: Together

1 Listening I'm here! ______ / 16

11 ▸ SB, pp. 148–151, p. 175

a) Read the exercise carefully. Then listen to two cousins, Oona and Fionn, talking on the phone. Tick (✓) the correct boxes. *(10 points)*

Transport:

Accommodation:

Oona and Lucy have...

	Yes	No
a double bed.		
twin beds.		
their own bathroom.		
their own shower.		
a kettle.		
Wi-Fi.		
a TV.		
a cooked breakfast.		

b) Listen again. Circle the correct answer – a), b) or c). *(6 points)*

1 Oona's journey took ...
- a) seven and a half hours.
- b) six and a half hours.
- c) one and a half hours.

2 Her accommodation in Belfast is ...
- a) not in a nice part of town.
- b) far from Fionn's house.
- c) not far from Fionn's house.

3 In her B&B, Oona can have tea ...
- a) with her breakfast.
- b) in her room.
- c) with her breakfast and in her room.

4 Oona and Fionn are going to see each other ...
- a) in the morning.
- b) in the afternoon.
- c) after the competition.

5 Oona's team are waiting for the judges to ...
- a) tell them when they can perform.
- b) tell them their score.
- c) give them the school address.

6 The aim for Oona's team is to ...
- a) have fun.
- b) beat the other teams.
- c) do well.

▸ Check

2 READING Life in Belfast ______ / 17

► SB, pp. 152–153, p. 176

Conor and Millie are visiting Belfast. Read about their day of sightseeing.

After breakfast, Conor and Millie went to the nice woman who ran their B&B.
'We have only one day in Belfast. What do you recommend?' Millie asked.
'The best way to learn about the city is to do a tour. You can do a black cab tour and learn about the Troubles, or there's a great tour of St George's Market, or if you like football, there's the stadium tour at Windsor Park,' she said and gave them some brochures.
'Look at these prices,' Conor said to Millie.
'We don't have enough money for this,' Millie said with a sad look. 'Let's just walk around.'
They walked to Victoria Square, where Millie noticed a bike stand with city bikes for hire.
'Who needs a tour guide? Let's go!' she said. The map on their phones told them that St George's Market wasn't far. They cycled there and walked through the busy market. They bought sweets at a stand and the friendly lady told them about the history of the market hall.
Back on their bikes, they decided to check out the National Football Stadium at Windsor Park. On the way they cycled past the Grand Opera House and then some colourful street art.
At the stadium, one of the gates was open, so they walked through to have a look. They watched the workers prepare the pitch. One of them took a break and Conor asked him some questions. He took them onto the pitch and showed them where famous players scored the greatest goals in the stadium's history. Finally they thanked him and said goodbye.

Next they decided to visit the Peace Wall on Shankill Road. There they cycled along the wall and photographed the murals, but soon it started to rain, so they went to a cafe.
An older man at the next table smiled at them and they chatted with him. He said as a child he and his brother made friends with two boys near Shankill Road. They played with them a lot and went to their houses and their mothers were very kind. Then one day a neighbour called to the two boys and said they shouldn't play with the brothers. Didn't they know that the boys were Catholics? After that the boys never played with him and his brother again. 'That's what growing up in Belfast was like,' the man said.
Back at the B&B, Conor and Millie told the manager about their day. She was surprised.
'Next time I'll tell my guests to hire bikes!'

a) **Number the places they visited in the right order. There's one place they didn't visit.** *(5 points)*

______ Windsor Park ______ Grand Opera House ______ Belfast Castle

______ St George's Market ______ Shankill Road ______ Victoria Square

b) **Complete the sentences.** *(12 points)*

1 The B&B manager ______________ several different ______________ to Conor and Millie.

2 They walked and ______________ because the tours were too ______________.

3 They learned about the market hall's ______________ from a lady at a ______________.

4 At Windsor Park, a ______________ took them on to the stadium's ______________.

5 At the Peace Wall they ______________ the murals until it began to ______________.

6 The man said the boys weren't ______________ to play with him and his ______________.

► Check

3 WORDS Trip to Northern Ireland ______/12

▶ SB, pp. 152–153, pp. 258–262

Jacob has posted a lot of photos from his family's trip to Belfast. Complete his texts with words from the box. There are two words you don't need.

abroad • age • B&B • cab • Catholic • confused • construction • divides • ID card • Protestant • recommended • routine • spectacular • time • the Troubles

I'm loving it here. It's the first (1) ______________ that I've been (2) ______________.

Northern Ireland isn't in the EU, so I had to show more than just an (3) ______________.

This is the (4) ______________ where we're staying.

They (5) ______________ a black (6) ______________ tour, so we took one. Very cool!

We learned that this Peace Wall (7) ______________ Protestant and (8) ______________ areas.

The street art shows how (9) ______________ are a big part of Belfast's history.

We went to the Titanic Museum. The (10) ______________ of the ship was amazing.

People told us we shouldn't miss this place. Now I know why. It's (11) ______________!

Is this Irish or Northern Irish culture? I'm still a little bit (12) ______________!

▶ Check

4 MEDIATION At a B&B ____/8

► SB, p. 151, p. 153, p. 177

You're visiting the Giant's Causeway, north of Belfast, with your family. You spend the night in a B&B near the coast. An older German couple arrives after you and you hear that they're having trouble communicating with the manager. You offer to help them.

Woman Ach, das ist ganz nett. Der junge Mann hat etwas von wegen twin beds gesagt. Ist das ein Doppelbett oder was ist der Unterschied?

You She would like to know (1) ______________________________

Manager Twin beds are two single beds. Some of our rooms have double beds, but unfortunately they are all booked at the moment.

You Er sagt, (2) ______________________________

Woman Ah, verstehe. Aber ein Zimmer mit twin beds ist perfekt. Das nehmen wir.

You She says (3) ______________________________

Manager Good. Could you complete this form, please? And I'll need to see your passports.

Woman Was sollen wir tun?

You Er möchte, dass Sie (4) ______________________________

____

Man Das kann ich machen. Eine kleine Frage: was kostet das Frühstück?

You (5) ______________________________

Manager A full cooked breakfast is included in the price.

You Er sagt, (6) ______________________________

Man Ach so! Na wunderbar. Und das Ganze kostet wieviel?

You (7) ______________________________

Manager All our rooms cost 80 pounds.

You (8) ______________________________

Man Alles klar. Das kriegen wir hin.

► Check

5 WRITING The big day ______/15

▸ More help, p. 77 ▸ SB, pp. 154–156, p. 180

Sophie took part in a dance competition. Look at the pictures and the words and phrases. Then tell the story in 70 words or more. Use linking words (*and, but, so, finally, …*) and time phrases (*every day, later, after that, …*). You can use the words under the pictures or your own ideas.

Remember: Geschichten erzählst du im *simple past*.

at home • competition • practice • routine

big day • bus • slowly • worried

competition • get off • hurry

arrive • late • not happy

big moment • nervous • on stage • perform • routine • watch

amazing day • announce • judges • surprised • winner

▸ Check

6 WORDS **Writing home** ____ / 10

► SB, pp. 150–151, p. 167, pp. 258–262

Naveed is travelling with a group in Northern Ireland. He writes an email home to his parents. Complete his email with words from the box. There are two more words than you need.

accommodation • bath • belong to • buffet • cereals • cold meats • cooked breakfast • form • guests • kettle • passport • twin beds

Erstelle dir beim Vokabeln lernen Wortfelder mit einem Oberbegriff, so kannst du dir neue Wörter besser merken.

to darya.azimi@example.net
from naveed.azimi@example.net

Hi Mum and Dad,

We arrived in Belfast last night! Our (1) ______________ here is much nicer than the last one. Ethan and I are still sharing a room, but now we have (2) ______________, so we can sleep better. Also, the room has a (3) ______________, so we can make tea. This morning I ate a full (4) ______________. It was really good! They also have a (5) ______________ with different things. You can have (6) ______________ like cornflakes as well as (7) ______________ and cheese with bread or toast. It's great! When we arrived last night, the lady at the desk asked us each to complete a (8) ______________ with our name and address. Then I showed her my ID card. Stupid me! We're not in the EU here, so I needed to show my (9) ______________. She said a lot of the (10) ______________ coming from Ireland make the same mistake. We're going to go sightseeing now. I'll write more later!

Love,
Naveed

Bereich	Aufgabe	erreichte Punktzahl	🤩	😎	🤔	😭
listening	1	____ / 16	16–15	14–12	11–8	7–0
reading	2	____ / 17	17–16	15–12	11–9	8–0
words	3 6	____ / 12 ____ / 10 } ____ /22	22–20	19–16	15–11	10–0
mediation	4	____ / 8	8	7–6	5–4	3–0
writing	5	____ / 15	15–14	13–11	10–8	7–0
Gesamt		____ / 78	78–71	70–55	54–39	38–0

More help

▶ Unit 1, page 11

7 WRITING A class trip ____ / 15

▶ SB. p. 27, p. 180

Write a blog post about a class trip that you have taken. Write 80 words or more.
- Find a title for your blog post
- Beginning: Introduce yourself and say where you went, when and for how long. Describe the weather.
- Middle: Pick three places/sights or activities and describe them. Make a new paragraph for each.
- End: Finish with a thought or message about your experience.

These questions can help you:
- How did you get there?
- How did you feel?
- Who was with you?
- Where did you stay (if you were there more than one day)?
- What did you do/see/watch?

You can use these words and phrases or your own:
Transport: bus • train • car • plane • ...
How long: for one/two/three/... days/nights/weeks
Weather: cold • warm • hot • sunny • cloudy • windy • rainy • ...
Places to stay: hotel • youth hostel • campsite • bed and breakfast • ...
Things to do: take a tour of ... • go to see ... • visit ... • watch • ...
Descriptions: amazing • big • cool • funny • great • modern • ...

You can start like this:

Hi everyone. My name is ______________________________

I want to tell you about ______________________________

We went for ______________________________

____

When we arrived ______________________________

____

Later ______________________________

____

If you want to go on a class trip, ______________________________

____

▶ Check

▶ Unit 2, page 19

8 WRITING Good advice ____ / 15

▶ SB, pp. 54–57, p. 180

You are helping with the advice column for your school's online student newspaper. Read the letter and give the student some advice. Write 80 words or more. You can use the phrases in the box to help you.

www.student.support.example.net

Dear advice column,

I have a classmate who I like and who I've wanted to be friends with, but he's never been interested. That's changed now. We're hanging out a lot and he's really nice to me. But here's the problem: I've heard that he has a crush on my sister. She's a year younger than us. If he's using me to get closer to my sister, then he's not really a friend. What can I do?

Unsure friend

Remember to:	You can use the phrases:
Thank him/her for the letter	Thank you for your letter. / ... writing to us. / ... writing to the advice column.
Say what the problem is	It's a bit strange that he ... • You want to trust him, but ... • If he ..., then maybe ... • You say that ...
Show understanding	I can see why you feel unsure about ... • I see why you need advice • I understand it's a difficult/an unhappy situation for you. • I understand why you don't feel good about ...
Give useful advice	Have you tried ...? • I think you should/shouldn't ... • Maybe you can ... • My advice would be to ... • Try to ... • You could ...
Say goodbye	Best wishes, / Good luck!

Dear Unsure friend,

____

____

____

____

____

____

____

____

▶ Check

▶ Unit 3, page 27

8 Writing Nessie on camera ____ / 15

▶ SB, pp. 82–85, p. 180

Last weekend the MacDonalds from Glasgow went camping at Loch Ness. Look at the pictures below. Write what happened to Iona, Jamie, Mr and Mrs MacDonald. Write 80 words or more. You can use words and phrases from the boxes below or your own ideas.

arrive • campsite • dinosaur • film • happy • look for • mobile phone • put up • secretly • show photos • surprised • tent • unpack **Linking words:** and • because • but • first, second, ... • however • so

In the afternoon the MacDonalds arrived at the campsite, ______

______

Later, ______

______

Jamie saw ______

______

In the evening, ______

______

The next day, ______

______

______

▶ Check

▶ Unit 4, page 59

8 WRITING A difficult question ____ / 15

▶ SB, pp. 124–127, p. 172, p. 180

You're emailing with your friend Malia. She's thinking about deleting her social media account after some negative experiences. Write an email and give your opinion. Include three good things and three bad things about social media and give reasons. Use opinion phrases. Write 80 words or more.

You can use the pictures for help. Use your own ideas too.

Good:

Bad:

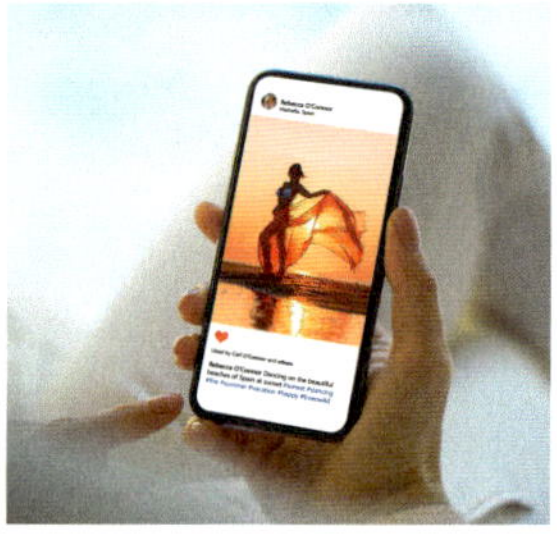

Opinion phrases: I believe ... • I think ... • If you ask me, ... • In my opinion ... • I'm not really a fan of ... • For me ... • I would say that ... • I think that's true/false. • I agree/don't agree with ...

You can start like this:

Hi Malia,
Here's what I think: ______________________________

____

First some of the good things: ______________________________

____

____

____

Some of the bad things are: ______________________________

____

____

____

Malia, I would say that ______________________________

____

____

▶ Check

▶ Unit 5, page 71

5 WRITING The big day ____/ 15

▶ SB, pp. 154–156, p. 180

Sophie took part in a dance competition. Look at the pictures and the words and phrases. Then tell the story in 70 words or more. You can use the words under the pictures or your own ideas.

Remember: Geschichten erzählst du im *simple past*.

every day • practice • routine • dance competition • at home

big day • dad • get on • bus • but • travel • slowly • worried

finally • get off • bus • hurry • competition

arrive • late • competition • door • not happy

then • big moment • come • nervous • everyone • watch • perform • routine • on stage

later • judges • announce • winner • surprised • win • amazing day

▶ Check

So bereitest du dich auf eine Arbeit vor

Damit du dich optimal auf eine Klassenarbeit vorbereiten kannst, musst du lernen, wie du richtig lernst. Das richtige Lernen bzw. Üben wird nicht von der Zahl der bearbeiteten Aufgaben, sondern viel mehr von der Lernatmosphäre und der Strukturierung des Lernprozesses, beeinflusst.

Die Lernatmosphäre vorbereiten

Eine ruhige, druckfreie Lernatmosphäre ist wichtig. Beim Lernen handelt es sich um eine bewertungsfreie Situation, in der das Üben im Vordergrund stehen soll. Es sollte dir möglich sein, angst- bzw. sorgenfrei **Fehler** zu machen und **Fragen** zu stellen. Dies ist wichtig für deinen Lernfortschritt.

Pausen gehören zum Lernprozess, denn sie helfen eine kognitive Überforderung zu verhindern. Auf eine 45-minütige Übungseinheit kann z.B. eine fünf- bis zehnminütige (Bewegungs-)Pause folgen.

Lerninhalte für die Klassenarbeit

Für eine erfolgreiche Vorbereitung ist es wichtig, die **Lerninhalte der Klassenarbeit** zu kennen. Du solltest dich daher mindestens eine Woche vor der Klassenarbeit bei der Fachlehrkraft informieren. Wenn du schon früher mit der Vorbereitung beginnen willst, kannst du im Inhaltsverzeichnis des Schülerbuchs (S. 4-9) nachschauen. Es besitzt eine ausführliche Übersicht über die Kompetenzen und sprachlichen Mittel (*vocabulary* & *grammar*), die du in jeder Unit vermittelt bekommst.

Ergänzende Materialien

Neben dem Klassenarbeitstrainer solltest du ein separates **Lernheft** führen. Dort kannst du die Arbeitsergebnisse zu den Aufgaben festhalten und so jede Aufgabe mehrfach bearbeiten.

Manchmal ist es ebenfalls hilfreich **eine Lernpartnerin oder einen Lernpartner** in der Klasse zu suchen. Ihr könnt euch unterstützen und bei Fragen und Problemen gegenseitig helfen.

Um keine der relevanten Kompetenzen zu vergessen, solltest du einen **Lernplan** erstellen. In diesem kannst du festhalten, was, wann geübt werden soll. Du kannst auch zusätzliche Übungsmöglichkeiten oder hilfreiche Schulbuchseiten notieren. Das Abhaken geübter Kompetenzen gibt dir einen Überblick über den Lernprozess bis zur Klassenarbeit. So könnte ein ausgefüllter Lernplan für Unit 3 aussehen:

Kompetenz / I can…	Sprachliche Mittel	Materialien	Wann übe ich das?	Erledigt?	Noch mal üben?
… talk about Scotland	Voc describing places	SB, p. 80–81 Vocabulary p. 239	Mo. 20.11.	✓	nein
… understand stories and legends	Voc ghost stories, legends, opinion phrases, …	SB, pp. 82–85 Wordbank, p. 204 Vocabulary, p. 239–241	Mo. 20.11.	✓	ja, am Do. 23.11.
… understand stories and legends	G adverbs of manner (revision)	G SB, p. 84 Language file, p. 190 Erklärfilm in der Cornelsen Lernen App	Di. 21.11.	✓	nein

Um dich gut auf die kommende Englischarbeit vorzubereiten, solltest du dich frühzeitig informieren, welche Themen in der Arbeit drankommen. Damit du nichts vergisst und auch genug Zeit hast, um zu lernen, solltest du dir einen Lernplan erstellen. Du kannst diesen Plan als Vorlage nutzen:

Lernplan von: ________________________________

Datum der Klassenarbeit: ________________________

Unit 1 / 2 / 3 / 4 / 5

Kompetenz / I can...	Sprachliche Mittel	Materialien	Wann übe ich das? (Datum)	Erledigt? (✓)	Noch mal üben? (ja/nein)

Cover

Cornelsen/li.: Shutterstock.com/Ron Ellis/courtesy of Transport for London; Personen: Chocolate Films; Hintergrund: re.: stock.adobe.com/anatoliycherkas

Illustrationen

Cornelsen/Gustavo Mazali (Beehive Illustration Agency): S. 9, S. 10, S. 13, S. 14, S. 15, S. 20/o., S. 21, S. 22, S. 27, S. 35, S. 37, S. 39, S. 55/r., S. 56, S. 64/o., S. 66, S. 70, S. 71, S. 75, S. 77; **Cornelsen/Irina Zinner**: S. 29

Abbildungen

S. 2: PEFC Deutschland e.V.; **S. 5**/2.v.o.: stock.adobe.com/Kaspars; S. 5/3.v.o.: Shutterstock.com/Fotimageon; S. 5/4.v.o.: stock.adobe.com/Tomas Marek; S. 5/o.: Shutterstock.com/S-F; S. 5/u.: Shutterstock.com/John McGreevy; **S. 6**/A: stock.adobe.com/adellyne; S. 6/B: stock.adobe.com/Mistervlad; S. 6/C: mauritius images/Andy Palmer/Alamy/Alamy Stock Photos; S. 6/D: stock.adobe.com/Iakov Kalinin; S. 6/E: stock.adobe.com/Tupungato; S. 6/F: stock.adobe.com/4kclips; **S. 7**: stock.adobe.com/peacefully; **S. 8**/r.: stock.adobe.com/chrisdorney; S. 8/Emoji m.: Shutterstock.com/Yefym Turkin; S. 8/Emoji u.: Shutterstock.com/Cali6ro; **S. 12**: Shutterstock.com/Yefym Turkin; **S. 16**/l.1+3: stock.adobe.com/Jacob Lund; S. 16/l.2+5: Shutterstock.com/Marian Fil; S. 16/l.4+6: Shutterstock.com/Torgado; S. 16/r.: stock.adobe.com/Glittering Humanity; **S. 17**/m.: Shutterstock.com/Eugenia Porechenskaya; S. 17/o.: stock.adobe.com/Xavier Lorenzo; S. 17/u.: Shutterstock.com/Shopping King Louie; **S. 18**: stock.adobe.com/denis_pc; **S. 20**/Emoji: Shutterstock.com/Yefym Turkin; **S. 23**/m.l.: stock.adobe.com/Daria Nipot; S. 23/m.m.: stock.adobe.com/Ralf; S. 23/m.r.: stock.adobe.com/gavin; S. 23/u.l.: stock.adobe.com/Nicola; S. 23/u.m.: stock.adobe.com/sablinstanislav; S. 23/u.r.: stock.adobe.com/Sebastian; **S. 24**: stock.adobe.com/Theerawat; **S. 26**: stock.adobe.com/Eberhard; **S. 28**/Emoji: Shutterstock.com/Yefym Turkin; S. 28/m.: stock.adobe.com/Stephen; **S. 31**: stock.adobe.com/peacefully; **S. 44**/A: Imago Stock & People GmbH/imago/PRiME Media Images; S. 44/B: stock.adobe.com/HildaWeges; S. 44/C: stock.adobe.com/Sebastian; S. 44/D: stock.adobe.com/Marcin; S. 44/E: stock.adobe.com/Alexey Fedorenko; S. 44/F: stock.adobe.com/Alexander; **S. 45**/Hand: stock.adobe.com/Lightwizard; S. 45/Power Button: stock.adobe.com/Ghori; **S. 51**/l.m.: stock.adobe.com/th-photo; S. 51/l.o.: stock.adobe.com/Soloviova Liudmyla; S. 51/l.u.: stock.adobe.com/Anze; S. 51/m.m.: mauritius images/Johnér; S. 51/m.o.: stock.adobe.com/Photobank; S. 51/m.u.: stock.adobe.com/Thomas Reimer; **S. 53**/A: Imago Stock & People GmbH/imago/PRiME Media Images; S. 53/B: stock.adobe.com/HildaWeges; S. 53/C: stock.adobe.com/Sebastian; S. 53/D: stock.adobe.com/Marcin; S. 53/E: stock.adobe.com/Alexey Fedorenko; S. 53/F: stock.adobe.com/Alexander; **S. 54**: stock.adobe.com/pisan; **S. 55**/Hand: stock.adobe.com/Lightwizard; S. 55/Power Button: stock.adobe.com/Ghori; **S. 57**: stock.adobe.com/Kien; **S. 58**: stock.adobe.com/PeterPike; **S. 59**/2.v.l.: Shutterstock.com/fizkes; S. 59/3.v.l.: stock.adobe.com/Kicking Studio; S. 59/l.: stock.adobe.com/Jade; S. 59/r.: stock.adobe.com/Darren Green; **S. 60**/Emoji: Shutterstock.com/Yefym Turkin; S. 60/o.: stock.adobe.com/dmutrojarmolinua; **S. 61**/A: mauritius images/EyeEm; S. 61/A: stock.adobe.com/susanne2688; S. 61/C: stock.adobe.com/salarko; S. 61/D: stock.adobe.com/hardyuno; S. 61/u.: Shutterstock.com/fizkes; **S. 62**/A: stock.adobe.com/BullRun; S. 62/B: stock.adobe.com/carballo; **S. 63**/l.2.v.o.: stock.adobe.com/Art_Photo; S. 63/l.3.v.o.: stock.adobe.com/perfectlab; S. 63/l.o.: stock.adobe.com/skif; S. 63/l.u.: stock.adobe.com/Laura; S. 63/m.m.: Imago Stock & People GmbH/MASKOT; S. 63/m.o.: stock.adobe.com/xavier gallego morel; S. 63/m.u.: stock.adobe.com/Valua Vitaly; S. 63/r.2.v.o.: stock.adobe.com/Rawpixel.com; S. 63/r.3.v.o.: Shutterstock.com/Prostock-studio; S. 63/r.o.: stock.adobe.com/Andrey Popov; S. 63/r.u.: stock.adobe.com/Ladanifer; **S. 64**/u.: stock.adobe.com/Monkey Business; **S. 65**/m.l.: stock.adobe.com/Soloviova Liudmyla; S. 65/m.m.: stock.adobe.com/Brocreative; S. 65/m.r.: stock.adobe.com/Lukasz Z; S. 65/o.l.: stock.adobe.com/auremar; S. 65/o.m.: Shutterstock.com/Odua Images; S. 65/o.r.: dpa Picture-Alliance/Design Pics; S. 65/u.: stock.adobe.com/fizkes; **S. 67**/m.l.: stock.adobe.com/th-photo; S. 67/m.m.: mauritius images/Johnér; S. 67/o.l.: stock.adobe.com/Soloviova Liudmyla; S. 67/o.m.: stock.adobe.com/Photobank; S. 67/u.l.: stock.adobe.com/Anze; S. 67/u.m.: stock.adobe.com/Thomas Reimer; **S. 68**: mauritius images/photononstop; **S. 69**/m.l.: mauritius images/Angela to Roxel/imageBROKER; S. 69/m.m.: mauritius images/robertharding; S. 69/m.r.: mauritius images/Ian Pilbeam/Alamy/Alamy Stock Photos; S. 69/o.l.: stock.adobe.com/Stephen Barnes, 2014; S. 69/o.m.: stock.adobe.com/filmbildfabrik; S. 69/o.r.: stock.adobe.com/Jeremy Francis; S. 69/u.l.: mauritius images/Hemis.fr; S. 69/u.m.: stock.adobe.com/Irina Schmidt; S. 69/u.r.: stock.adobe.com/Regina; **S. 72**: Shutterstock.com/Yefym Turkin; **S. 76**/2.v.l.: Shutterstock.com/fizkes; S. 76/3.v.l.: stock.adobe.com/Kicking Studio; S. 76/l.: stock.adobe.com/Jade; S. 76/r.: stock.adobe.com/Darren Green